Heidi may the magic
of the fairies always be
with you.

Scarletina's Quest
for Fairy Wings

....

THE EARTH CIRCLE

Bess Drew Sherret

Bess Drew Sherret

FriesenPress

Suite 300 – 990 Fort Street
Victoria, BC, Canada V8V 3K2
www.friesenpress.com

Copyright © 2014 by Bess Drew Sherret
First Edition — 2014

All rights reserved.

ISBN
978-1-4602-5094-5 (Hardcover)
978-1-4602-5095-2 (Paperback)
978-1-4602-5096-9 (eBook)

1. Juvenile Fiction, Science Fiction, Fantasy, Magic

Distributed to the trade by The Ingram Book Company

Table of Contents

Foreword

Scarletina's Quest for Fairy Wings is the first of an enchanted saga – which could even hold the secret into gaining your very own wings of life.

Author, Bess Drew Sherret, has spent most of her years as an actress – also telling endless stories, without even stopping for a breath. Consequently, her animated way with words, will play like a 3D movie in your head. Her creatures and colourful worlds, dance deliciously through your imagination,

Scarletina has been a lifetime in the making. This thoughtful little fairy, has always sat upon Bess's shoulder, until it was time for her to burst onto the page, with a loud splatter!

Most of all, this is a story that will not leave you cowering under the covers. There is nothing to fear in this fairytale.

To all eager readers, it will encourage a fearless excitement, as this purposeful tale is woven with precious

teachings of the world and its inhabitants. You will never look at an insect nor a flower or star again, without wonder and appreciation. Everything and everyone has an important life-task to complete.

There are consequences and lessons to be learnt for every happy ending, even for us Two-Leggeds!

Join Scarletina, as she develops into the most mischievous, kind and clever little fairy, that ever fluttered. Even her name is a collision of naughty and nice.

Move over Tinkerbell, Scarletina of Nightingale Wood is here, to take you with her, on her spellbinding adventures.

Tessa Edwardes

GradDip J – from University of Canterbury, NZ.

Freelance writer/journalist.

Chapter One
Detention

Scarletina's mother called out to her, "Hurry up or you will be late for school!"

Leaping onto another leaf, Scarletina shook her wet hair and giggled as she scattered rainbow water droplets from her fingertips. "Thank you, Water Bringers, for my shower. I feel much better now."

"Scarletina, I don't want to have to call you again!"

Her mother's voice had that cross sound to it. Scowling from underneath damp eyelashes, Scarletina unwillingly replied, "Alright, Mother. Coming." A deep sigh escaped from her; she really didn't want to start Earth school again. Going to school meant she wouldn't be able to spend the days with her friends, exploring and having adventures in the woods. Why did things have to change? Why did she even have to go back to school? What was the point?

 1

"Quickly, Scarletina, hurry and get dressed or you will miss your ride!" scolded her mother.

"Alright, but why do I have to go to the Earth Circle? I mean I can learn just as much here with you. I discover a lot in the Dark Time of Winter, when the Circle is sealed and closed."

Pulling Scarletina to her, so they were looking into each other's eyes, her mother said firmly, "There are things that your father and I cannot teach you. You must understand, little one, that some learning has to be done with others; that's our way. That is why the time is shared between the Circles and your home. Both have their own unique knowledge to give, and you have to tread this path, Scarletina, if you want to get your wings." With a gentle push her mother urged her to get dressed.

Angrily, Scarletina went into the room where she slept, and picked up a tunic from the floor. She had worn it the day before, but it would save her time looking for a clean one. After all, she had only worn it for one day.

Grabbing her packed lunch from the table, she quickly kissed her mother goodbye. Pausing at the doorway, Scarletina placed her hand on the entrance to their home. "Thank you, Shard, for allowing me to live within you," whispered Scarletina. She then placed her forehead on the sacred spot as many had done before.

No matter how busy, cross, or tired she was, Scarletina never forgot to offer her gratitude, and thanks, to the giant oak. No one ever took for granted the shelter it gave to them and their families. Scarletina had been taught to do this by her parents as they had been by theirs. They were the Oak-Dwellers and they had been sheltered in this same tree for many lifetimes. Their family name was Sharder, because every family that lived within an oak always took its name.

Her mother called out, "Have a good day, Scarletina. Try not to be late for school."

"Bye, Mother. I will go as quickly as I can." Scarletina called out as she raced down the sturdy arms of the tree.

As she neared the edge of the branch, she was relieved to see her lift was waiting patiently for her. Scarletina loved her Guardian, and cheerfully waved to her. Each of Suntra-Spider's eight legs motioned back. The spider's brown colouring made her almost invisible. It was only because this is where they met every day that Scarletina could spot her.

Scarletina curtsied. "I offer you Greetings of the Day Suntra-Spider. Will you take me down, so that I may attend the Earth Circle, please?"

The spider said nothing, and all of her legs were still. She was staring at Scarletina who shifted uncomfortably under Suntra-Spider's steady gaze. The spider started spinning and her delicate threads glistened and shone as she worked. Scarletina wondered what was happening. Usually, she climbed onto the back of her friend, who then spun a single thread, allowing them to travel down to the earth level.

Scarletina anxiously asked, "Please, Suntra-Spider, take me down. I can hear the toning of the bell, which means the Circle will be starting soon. We have to go now if I am to get there in time."

"The answer is in my woven web. Can't you read it?" Suntra-Spider's silky soft and gentle voice replied.

"No, of course not. We learn web reading when we are in the Moon Circle. You know that," Scarletina crossly retorted.

"Ah, yes! The Earth Circle has to be completed before you can graduate to the Moon Circle. Tell me, little one, do you want to be able to read my webs, to learn about our way of life?" the spider asked.

"Yes, I do, but Suntra-Spider, please take me down. If I am late, our teacher, Tutty-Grandhill, will be very cross with me."

"So," Suntra Spider asked, "You do think it's worth missing fun times with your friends to become a Fully-Fledged Fairy, then?"

Scarletina was startled. She realised the spider had picked up on her inner thoughts that morning. How could she do that?

Suntra-Spider spoke with pride in her voice, "We, of the Spider-clans, listen to thoughts and feel vibrations through the hairs on our bodies. That is how we protect and nurture the Fairy commune. Until you can fly, you must have a protector to watch over you in case you get into trouble. You have much to learn in the Circles, Scarletina. Now, stop looking so scared; I will not tell anyone about your rebellious thoughts. We are also the Keeper of Secrets. Come on, up on my back."

Suntra-Spider's deep chuckle rumbled within her, and tickled Scarletina's legs. "Oh, but your face was so funny to see, little one. So funny to see."

Swiftly, they descended arriving with hardly a bump, "Thank you, Suntra-Spider, for the ride, and for the teaching."

The spider softly tapped the top of Scarletina's head with one of her long legs. "Off you go. I'll be waiting here for you when the Circle is finished to take you home. You may not have noticed, but I went for a very fast descent today, so you have some extra time. You won't have to run. Scarletina, always try to listen with an open heart and mind."

"Thank you, Suntra-Spider. I thought you were moving very fast today," giggled Scarletina. "I will try to be good. I promise."

As she reached the Place of Decision, she saw her best friend, Shantreel who lived a few oaks away from Shard. Shantreel's family name was Oak-Fadder, and Scarletina thought her the cleverest and prettiest fairy in the Circle. Today, Shantreel was wearing a green tunic with small wisps of moss on the hem. Her long blonde hair was entwined with vine leaves, and tiny tendrils curled around her face. Not only was she very pretty, but she had the sweetest of natures. She was the voice of reason to the often impetuous Scarletina.

"I offer you Greetings of the Morning, Scarletina."

They greeted in the way of the Cropplets, the name for the Earth students. Scarletina and Shantreel placed the first two fingers of their right hand onto their right closed eyelid. Then the two fingers of their left hand were gently placed on the other's closed left eyelid. Great care had to be taken not to injure one another. This had been the first lesson they had learnt in the Earth Circle because it showed trust in each other. The greeting ended by hugging one another.

As they drew apart, Shantreel shrieked, "Goodness, how have you managed to get a mark on your dress already?"

"What! Where?" Scarletina screamed in dismay when she saw the large brown stain right in the middle of her tunic. "Oh no! I must have done that last evening when I was playing in the woods."

"You didn't put on a fresh tunic? You are asking for trouble! You know how strict Tutty-Grandhill is about always looking clean and tidy! And it looks like you didn't even brush your hair this morning," said Shantreel.

Scarletina hated her hair. Not only was it bright red, but most hateful of all was that it was incredibly curly. No amount of pulling and tugging ever straightened it. To get it looking even a little presentable meant hundreds of brush strokes!

Scarletina's voice trembled as she replied, "I didn't have time to do it this morning! Well, I can't do anything about it now. Maybe she won't notice the stain or my hair?"

Shantreel could tell her friend was very frightened. Tutty-Grandhill could be fearsome when she was cross. Taking her friends hand to comfort her, she asked, "Which pathway are we going to take to the Earth Circle?"

"The quickest way is through the Mushroom Tunnels, though it is dark in there, isn't it? Although it takes a little bit longer, I prefer Fernshade Walk, but do we have time?" asked Scarletina.

"Yes, we do, but only if we walk quickly. Okay, let's go along Fernshade Walk, but no stopping to play with the Ant-Builders, Scarletina, okay?"

Scarletina nodded her agreement, "Promise me, Scarletina," Shantreel insisted.

Hooking her two thumbs together, which made her hands look like wings, Scarletina placed them against her chest and said, "I promise I will not stop to play, or talk, to the Ant-Builders."

Shantreel was satisfied as no-one, ever, broke their promise after taking the Winged-Oath. Happily taking her friend's hand, they started to walk along their chosen path. Both of them loved the covered walk as the sun filtered through the tall ferns making shadow patterns on the earth.

Suddenly, they heard an Ant-Builder saying, "We offer you Greetings of the Morning, Cropplets. Why not stay awhile and talk with us?"

Shantreel squeezed Scarletina's hand in a warning gesture. She knew the Ant-Builders never paused in their work. If they wanted to chat, you had to keep pace with them. You had to go where they did. This led to lots of surprises and adventures, which is why Scarletina loved spending time with them. They showed her secret places that only Ant-Builders could find. No matter how many times she walked a path with them, Scarletina said she never found it again on her own. The Ant-Builders were clever, and twisted and turned so their ways remained secret.

"We offer you Greetings of the Morning, Ant-Builders, but I am sorry, we cannot stop today. We must hurry or we'll be late for the Circle," Scarletina explained.

"Oh dear, Tutty-Grandhill is fearsome when she gets cross isn't she! Hurry, then, hurry! Make haste as we do. Do not falter, linger, or stop... Hurry... Hurry..." chorused the Ant-Builders as they disappeared along a hidden pathway.

"Nearly there, Scarletina. Come on, we can't slow down," Shantreel urged.

"I have a pain in my side. I need to stop," pleaded Scarletina.

"You will feel the pain of Tutty-Grandhill's tongue if we are late. That would be far worse than the ache you are moaning about. Come on!" Shantreel knew her friend was trying to delay her arrival at the Circle. She understood that Scarletina was dreading the teacher seeing her stained tunic and unkempt hair.

No Cropplet had ever seen Tutty-Grandhill with even a hair out of place. Even when she had been flying, her hair always looked perfect. It was the colour of a storm-filled sky, dark grey flecked with silver flashes. She always wore it in a plait loosely curled around at the top of her head. Her eyes were the colour of bluebells, which darkened when she was cross. Shantreel knew that her teacher's eyes would be very dark when she looked at Scarletina today!

They arrived just as the bell stopped its slow pealing. Silence reigned. All the students stood by their desks waiting for Tutty-Grandhill to make her entrance. This was usually Scarletina's favourite part of the day.

Her teacher's aerial skills were renowned for their daring, and unique movements. These skills were much talked about by the fairies of Nightingale Wood. They often wondered why she was not in the Sun Circle where students learnt to fly. When Scarletina had asked her mother about this, she had been told that each teacher had a choice of which Circle to go to. Obviously, Tutty-Grandhill preferred the Earth Circle.

Scarletina found this quite hard to understand. How could someone prefer to be down on the ground and not up in the air? Why would Tutty-Grandhill not want to teach flying? Scarletina felt there was more to this than her mother was telling her.

It was the rush of air blowing on the students cheeks that heralded the arrival of Tutty-Grandhill. Eyes searched the sky and trees to get that first glimpse.

There she was! Scarletina's heart raced along with all the other Cropplets as they watched her soaring high, then diving low. Holding their breath as they watched her skimming over the tree tops. Gasping in admiration as she spun around so fast, she became a blur. Then, suddenly, she was totally still. Her wings didn't move. Other fairies hovered, but Tutty-Grandhill just stopped! She was suspended in mid-air. Then, slowly, and gracefully, she descended into the Circle, delicately landing on the soft mossy floor.

"I offer you Greetings of the Day, Cropplets," Tutty-Grandhill's soft voice was very different from the gaze that scanned every student. Her piercing eyes never ever missed a thing!

Scarletina watched as those eyes came closer to looking at her. She knew she was in trouble! Her heart was filled with dread, which made it beat very fast, and there wasn't anything she could do to stop it.

The dreaded moment arrived as Tutty-Grandhill looked at Scarletina. Her eyes went first to the mop of disheveled red hair. Then, it slowly travelled down her tunic coming to rest on the telltale stain. "Tut...Tut...Tut...Tut"

When that dreaded sound was heard, it showed Tutty-Grandhill was very displeased. Everyone held their breath. Scarletina felt her face go as red as her hair. Her mouth felt very dry, but her hands were sweaty.

"Why have you come to the Circle with your clothes in such a disgraceful state?" demanded Tutty-Grandhill.

Scarletina felt her fellow Cropplets eyes boring into her. She did not dare look around to see if this were true, for to turn away from Tutty-Grandhill at this moment was certain to encourage further wrath.

"I offer my regrets for this lack of proper attire, but I..." Scarletina hesitated. What could she say? What excuse could she give?

"Come to my table when you have an explanation, but do not make me wait too long for you! While I am waiting for Scarletina's reasons for her disgraceful attire, I would like all the other Cropplets to be seated, and prepare for today's lessons"

Scarletina's mind raced as she tried to think what excuse she might give. She could say she had tripped and fallen on the way to school, or explain she had picked up the wrong tunic because she had been late, and in her haste had chosen the dirty one, instead of the clean one. Yes, that is what she would say. That sounded really good!

As she approached Tutty-Grandhill, her heart stopped when she saw Stupple-Spider standing beside her teacher, who was now seated at her table.

With dread in her heart, she remembered the conversation with Suntra-Spider that morning. What was she to do? Stupple-Spider would know she was telling a lie! To tell an untruth was considered one of the worst offences resulting in a permanent bad mark on your report card. The voice of fear in her head told her to go ahead with the lie. After all, Suntra-Spider had said they were also the Keeper of Secrets. So, Stupple-Spider wouldn't be able to say anything, would she?

Scarletina stood trembling before her teacher. What was she going to do? Taking a deep breath she said, "I was in a very bad mood this morning because I didn't want to come to the Earth Circle. I wanted to play in the woods, but my mother insisted that I attend. I felt angry about this, so I couldn't be bothered to look for a clean tunic or brush my hair."

Once again, the piercing eyes of Tutty-Grandhill bored into her. "Thank you for your honesty, Scarletina.

Bess Drew Sherret

It cannot have been easy for you to confess your bad-tempered mood to us all. Whilst we are glad you chose to come to class, to show such disrespect to the Earth Circle is a serious offence. As a punishment, you will not be joining us this afternoon when we go to the Sun Circle to watch the first unassisted flight of Fairy-Gamalan. This is a special event, and Cropplets are given this opportunity to show that with hard work and a willing heart that they, too, one day will reach this pinnacle. To attend such an occasion in stained attire and unkempt hair would be disrespectful. I am sure you agree?"

Scarletina's eyes prickled with unshed tears; she would miss seeing Fairy-Gamalan! She had been looking forward to this special treat for weeks now. To watch a fairy flying solo for the first time, unassisted, was magical and nerve-racking. Scarletina brushed away the tears and said, "I agree that my dress would not show the proper respect for such an occasion. Had I remembered about Fairy Gamalan, I would have put on a clean tunic."

"It is a hard price for you to pay Scarletina, yet I feel that you will have learnt a valuable lesson. That lesson is that we cannot predict what might happen. We cannot ever be sure that our day is going to be as we planned or the same as our yesterday. The only constant thing in our lives is change. I want you all to remember this. We will be leaving soon, but we still have time to continue our lessons about the creatures that share Nightingale

Wood with us. Today, I thought we would talk about the Ant-Builders."

It was a subdued and red-faced Scarletina who returned to her seat. Her heightened colour revealed how embarrassed she felt at being chastised in front of her fellow Cropplets. Yet, when she stole a sideways glance, the eyes that looked back at her were filled with sympathy. They knew she would be dismayed, to be missing the spectacular event of a first unassisted flight. Once she was seated back in her chair, Tutty-Grandhill began the class.

"I was telling you yesterday the importance of respecting all forms of creatures, the way they live, and how we can come to understand them by studying their way of life. This also gives us wonderful opportunities to see how they behave, and what we may learn from them. It is extremely important to remember not to interfere with the many creatures that are part of our lives in Nightingale Wood. We must never cause them any pain or stress, but offer to help them if they are in trouble. In the Moon Circle, this will become easier as you will be taught to communicate with them. This is vital for the continued peaceful existence in our woods. We are going to talk about the very busy Ant-Builders. What do you think they can teach us? Have any of you had a chance to speak to them?"

There was a general shaking of heads and murmuring, "What are you whispering about, Cropplets?" asked Tutty-Grandhill.

Shantreel said, "I know that Scarletina has spoken to the Ant-Builders many times. In fact, today, they wanted her to stop and talk with them. She refused as she didn't want to be late for the Circle."

"So, you are well acquainted with them, Scarletina. Perhaps you would like to tell the class about your experiences?" Tutty-Grandhill accompanied the request with a smile, and gestured for Scarletina to come out to the front.

This was the last thing that Scarletina wanted to happen. She was still feeling upset, and somewhat troubled by everything that had happened. She had been hoping that once the other Cropplets had gone to the Sun Circle, she would be able to go home. What she needed now was the peace and comfort of her own bed. Instead, she was being asked to stand up in front of the class and talk about her Ant-Builder friends as though nothing awful had happened!

The silence, as her teacher waited for Scarletina's response, was broken by the sounds of the world outside the Circle. Birds whistled and chirruped, frogs croaked, and butterflies whispered with their wings. This gladdened Scarletina; she felt they understood how she was feeling. Then she heard the woodland creatures calling out to her, " Don't be too downhearted," whispered the butterflies. " Come on. Put aside how you're feeling," croaked the frogs. "Share your adventures with the Ant-Builders," whistled the birds.

Scarletina realised it was because of her own bad temper that she had been chastised in front of everyone. Yet, it could be worse; it wasn't the end of the world. She hadn't lied! She had told the truth and faced her fears. She would take some comfort in that. A very good lesson had been learnt: she must control her temper and make sure she came to school properly dressed.

Scarletina smiled back at her teacher and said, "I would be very happy to share my adventures, Tutty-Grandhill."

The class was spellbound and enthralled as they listened about her first meeting with the Ant-Builders. "I was collecting dried grass to make a basket when I heard singing." Scarletina giggled, "Well, it wasn't really singing as we know it, rather, a warbling sound, some high, others low. I was looking around to see what was making the noise when suddenly out of the grasses came the Ant-Builders. Each of them carrying something and moving very fast. I asked them where they were going, and they told me they were moving their home to a warmer spot in the woods."

"Did they stop and talk to you, Scarletina? I mean, did one stop, or did they all?" asked one of the students.

"They didn't stop at all! I had to keep up with them and talk at the same time. The long line of ants went as far back as I could see. They are so determined; they don't stop for any obstacles, no matter how big they might be. The Ant-Builders just go around or over them. When they move from one place to another, every ant carries something to the new site. When that is done, they race back to get more. I got talking to one of them. She introduced herself as A141. They don't have names, just numbers as there are too many of them," Scarletina explained.

"You said she introduced herself, Scarletina. How do you know it wasn't a male ant?" another Cropplet asked.

"Because she told me that every female is a worker ant, whereas the male's job is to protect and look after their Queen," Scarletina responded.

"Cropplets, I expect that surprises you, doesn't it? That only the females ants are the workers, and the male ants guard and serve their Queen? This is a very good example for you; it shows how life forms have their own way of working things out to suit them and their lives," commented Tutty-Grandhill. "Tell me, Scarletina, how many times have you met with the Ant-Builders?"

"About four times now, I think. I have to wait until they want to meet me; I cannot go to them, for I do not know where their home is. When I travel with them, they twist and turn so much that I have no idea whereabouts we are in the wood. A141, or her friend, A426, always has to guide me back to the pathway," confessed Scarletina.

"Can you say you have learnt anything from the Ant-Builders?" asked one of the students named Abradina.

"Thank you for asking me that question, Abradina. I've never thought about that before. The first thing is how motivated they are. Nothing can deter them from reaching their goal. Whatever is put in their way, they go around or over it; they work together as a team. I am sure there will be lots more examples that I will see in the future, but that is what I have seen so far," Scarletina replied.

"Thank you for telling us about your experiences, Scarletina; it was extremely interesting. It is almost lunch time, so I suggest everyone, except Scarletina, collect their packed lunches, and we will eat them at the Sun Circle. I think we should show our appreciation to Scarletina for a very interesting and informative insight into the world of the Ant-Builders."

Tutty-Grandhill led the class in the typical fairy way of showing their thanks; everyone raised their arms above their heads, hands clasped together, with their fingers intertwined. Then they rocked their enclosed hands back and forth whilst chanting Choo-Hah Choo-Hah Choo-Hah. A blushing Scarletina responded with the Fairy Thank You. She placed her wrists together and tapped her fingers against each other, then bowed her head three times.

Scarletina felt very sad and regretful as she watched her friends depart to the Sun Circle. Everyone was so excited about seeing an unassisted flight and, of course, it meant no more school for them that day.

Tutty-Grandhill had told Scarletina to stay in the classroom and write two pages on the importance of dressing correctly when attending the Circle and, also, what she would miss most about not attending the Sun Circle .

Stupple-Spider would stay in the classroom until Scarletina had finished the task that had been given to her, and only then would she be allowed to go home. Tutty-Grandhill also added, "If you haven't completed it by the time school is finished, Scarletina, then you will have to stay behind tomorrow to finish it. If that is the case, then do not forget to tell your mother that you will be home a little late, so she won't worry."

Scarletina didn't want to have to stay late the next day. That would mean her mother would know about her punishment. Pushing her thoughts aside, she started writing about the episode, and strangely enough it helped her realise how silly she had been. Her temper tantrum had stopped her from sharing a wonderful time with fellow Cropplets at the Sun Circle. It also had caused her much embarrassment as no one likes to be told off in front of their friends.

Scarletina was so engrossed in her task that she was completely unaware that it was time to go home. She was surprised when Stupple-Spider tapped her on the shoulder, "Scarletina, Suntra-Spider is waiting by the Ancient One. It is time for her to take you home. Have you finished the work Tutty-Grandhill gave you?"

"Nearly. Just a few more lines to write, and then I will be done. I would have been happy to have walked back to Shard tonight, Stupple-Spider. I always love walking through the woods when I am feeling a little sad; I find it helps me."

"When we are on our own, feeling unhappy, and our spirits are low, we are not at our most observant, Scarletina. We always have to be on our guard in the woodlands; not everything is our friend. The humans, those we call the Two-Leggeds, come to walk our pathways as the Giver of SunLight and Warmth goes to sleep. Nightfall changes the woodland; things look different in the dark. You must be extra careful when they are around. Remember, you cannot fly out of peril, can you? They cannot see us. We are so tiny compared to them. Even a fully grown fairy is only as big as one of the largest fingers on their hands. We can so easily be crushed beneath their feet. Scarletina, we, your elders, are responsible for your well-being. We are wiser in the ways of life. So, please, listen and remember what I have said to you today."

Scarletina could listen to Stupple-Spider forever, her voice was gentle and kind, and she always spoke such wise and meaningful words. But she never came across as being bossy, which is why everyone in the Earth Circle loved her so much.

"My heartfelt thanks for your wisdom, Stupple-Spider. I would not have thought about that at all, and you are right, the woods can be a frightening place sometimes," confessed Scarletina.

"Off you go then, see you tomorrow, in a clean tunic Scarletina!" Stupple-Spiders laughter sounded the same as when raindrops fell on Shards leaves. Scarletina waved her goodbye and hastened to The Ancient One.

Chapter Two
Confessions

"Scarletina, come and help me with Fairy-Gamalan's gift."

"What are you making for her, Mother?" Scarletina asked.

"Spinny-Spider, at my request, spun a pair of wing covers for Fairy-Gamalan. She has her measurements for the gown she is working on for her Ascension of Wings Ceremony. So it will be a surprise for her, when she receives our gift."

"Why do we need wing covers, mother. I mean, what do they do?" asked a puzzled Scarletina.

"When our wings are new we have to be very careful as they are quite fragile, and can be a bit wobbly in places. We can easily catch them on bushes, or get them burnt by the hot rays from the Giver of SunLight and Warmth. We wear our covers until our wings are nice and firm, and no longer in danger of being damaged. When we are first learning to fly, the wing covers do not need to be removed as we only go for short trips with a Huffler. For the unassisted flight, they are removed as we fly much higher and stay aloft a lot longer," her mother responded.

"What is a Huffler?" asked a puzzled Scarletina as she had never heard that word before.

"That is the name given to the fairies who teach us to fly. My one was called Huffler-Featherdown because she seemed to float just like a feather. You could hardly see her wings moving."

"But wasn't the unassisted flight celebrated today? Aren't we late with the gift?" asked Scarletina.

"No, because today Fairy-Gamalan would still have had a Huffler flying alongside her. She is unassisted because her hand is not being held. On the day of the Ascension of Wings Ceremony, she will fly on her own, with no one to help her if she gets into trouble. How did Fairy Gamalan do today? Was she pleased with her flight?" asked her mother.

Scarletina had deliberately kept herself busy since returning from the Circle, to avoid having to tell her mother she had not gone to watch the unassisted flight and, more importantly, why she had not been allowed to go see Fairy-Gamalan. Her mother would be very cross if she were to find out what had happened. Scarletina knew her mother would write about it in the Family Life Journal where she recorded the events of the day.

When her father returned home from his visit to the Gathering of the Elementals, she knew he would look at the journal. He always enjoyed reading about the things that had happened whilst he was away. There had been six risings of the Giver of SunLight and Warmth since he had left, and he was expected back anytime.

"Scarletina, did you hear me?" her mother asked.

"I didn't go to the Ascension Circle, Mother," mumbled Scarletina.

Her mother looked shocked and asked, "Not go! I don't understand! Tutty-Grandhill informed us that all of the Cropplets would be going there for the afternoon. Why didn't you go?"

The lump of fear in Scarletina's throat seemed huge. Surely, no words could pass through it. She swallowed hard, but it wouldn't go away. Her heart was beating so fast, thump... thump...thumpity thump! It was so loud she could hear it, so perhaps her mother could, too?

Looking up through lowered lashes, she saw her mother didn't appear to be troubled in any way. Just looking at her, waiting for an answer to her question. Scarletina's eyes filled with unshed tears, then, slowly, one tear escaped and trickled down her cheek. This was quickly followed by another, then another. Soon many tears were racing down her face, and splashing onto her hands, a frightened sob escaped before she could hold it in.

   Bess Drew Sherret

Suddenly, she was enveloped in her mother's arms, "Whatever is it, Scarletina? It isn't like you to cry. What has happened? Surely, it can't be that bad?" her mother asked.

Scarletina's muffled response was just loud enough for her mother to hear, "Oh, Scarletina, this will be a bad mark in your school report. If you get too many, then you run the risk of staying in the Earth Circle for a very long time. When are you going to grow up and start behaving like a Cropplet? Your father will be as disappointed in you as I am. Because of your bad attitude, you missed a really fun time. I hope you have learnt a lesson from this episode?"

Looking up at her mother she confessed "I have. I felt silly and stupid having to explain myself in front of the class. It made me seem very childish. Then being banned from seeing Fairy-Gamalan's flight with everyone else, was just…" Scarletina buried her head as the tears started to flow again.

Her mother gently wiped Scarletina's face saying, "Alright, little one, stop crying now, or your eyes will be red and sore. Then you won't be able to see out of them to help me with Fairy-Gamalan's gift."

"What will Father say? I expect he will be cross with me," asked a worried Scarletina.

Her mother reassured her, "He won't be cross with you. I'll tell him you know you have learnt a valuable lesson, and realise how stupidly you behaved. You will have to prove that to us, though, Scarletina, by your behaviour in the future, won't you."

"Oh, yes, I will, Mother. I don't want to go through another day like I had today. Is it time to check the oak leaf on the Daykeeper?" Scarletina asked.

"Yes, and remember only one more day till it is time for you to put them back in their box, and take out the Royal Oak leaves. You mustn't forget, Scarletina. I am depending on you." Her mother urged.

Scarletina knew she would never forget to complete the ritual of the Daykeeper. She had been honoured when her parents had given her this important task to do. When her parents began their married life in the oak tree, Shard had given them a strong, slim branch, that had seven leaves on it. This was to be their Daykeeper.

Her parents had carefully removed the seven oak leaves and taken them to the Spider-Spinners. A strong but light protective covering was woven by the Spider-Spinners, and placed over each of the leaves. Five were marked with the Silver Star symbol; these were known as the Quintuple Stars. The sixth had a Silver Crown and the seventh a Gold Crown. These two were known as the Royal Crowns.

Every newlywed couple went through this ritual, for this was how the fairies marked the days. The five Silver Star leaves represented the days that Fully-Fledged

🍀   *Bess Drew Sherret*

Fairies went to work, and children attended The Circles. The leaves marked with the Silver and Gold Crowns were family time, days when they were free to do as they wished. Also, they were for those special occasions that the fairy commune celebrated together. The leaves were treasured by every family, and kept in a polished wooden box that was painted with magical symbols. The box was always a gift from the magical Abra Clan.

It was Scarletina's duty to ensure that either the five Silver Stars, or the two Royal Crown leaves were on the DayKeeper. The leaves glowed a deep blue when they were placed onto the branch. Scarletina's job was to move a leaf to the Day-Beginning marker. Then, the leaves would magically move along the DayKeeper, until they reached the Day-Ending marker, where they turned a bright gold.

Once all Quintuple Stars, the five Silver Star leaves had been used, they were taken from the branch, and placed in the polished wooden box, with magical symbols on. Then the Royal Crowns, the Silver and Gold Royal leaves were taken out, and placed on the DayKeeper.

This was an important task; chaos would result if she forgot to change the leaves over as it marked the beginning of family and work times.

There was a story that was told at the Earth Circle about a young Cropplet, who hadn't taken her task too seriously. One time she failed to change the leaves from the Quintuple Stars to the Royal Crowns. This resulted in the whole family missing the ceremony of the Blessing and Crowning of the King and Queen, bringing disgrace and sadness to her whole family.

When this story was told at the Earth Circle, the shocked expressions on the Cropplets faces showed how such a failure was regarded. Apart from missing the spectacular event of the Blessing and Crowning of the King and Queen, the family were absent from the event without permission. This was seen as a lack of respect, and could have resulted in them being banished from the fairy commune. Apparently, the Cropplet, realising what she had done, had become afraid and fled from Nightingale Wood. Thankfully, her Guardian from the Spider-Clan followed her, and found the Cropplet curled up on a bed of leaves. The Cropplet was brought back home, and later the King and Queen pardoned the whole family. The story was told as a warning to those who took on the very important job of DayKeeper.

Holding up the finished wing covers, Scarletina's mother asked, "Do you think I have embroidered on enough StarDust?"

"Oh, Mother, it is beautiful! Fairy-Gamalan will be thrilled. It must be very hard to sew on the StarDust. How do you do it?" asked Scarletina.

"Come and sit by me," said her mother, " I think this will be a very good time, while your Father is away, to explain how important embroidery is to us fairy folk."

Scarletina was thrilled for the chance to learn about fairy embroidery. Usually such matters were only shared during the dark and cold time of Winter. That's when all the Circles were sealed and closed, until the coming of the New Leaves in Spring.

The students always looked forward to this time as it meant they didn't have to go to school. More important to them than having this freedom, was learning about their families and their ancestors. The sharing of this knowledge was never ignored, or overlooked; it meant honouring, and respecting your family by remembering them. This ensured they were never forgotten, and would remain forever in their families' thoughts and hearts.

Settling herself down next to her mother, Scarletina could hardly contain her excitement. Her eyes were glued to her mother's face, she was very happy to have this special time together.

"The embroidery stitches that I sew on our clothes, and that adorn things in our home, tell about our ancestry, our family stories, and our history here in Nightingale Wood. There are fairy communes all over the world, and they also use embroidery to tell about their way of life. We are all different from each other, so we have our own unique stories to remember. You will learn all about the many Worldwide Fairy Clans in the Moon Circle, so I will not talk about them today as it would take far too long. We could be here for hours!" her mother laughed.

Picking up the wing covers, her mother said, "You see how I have embroidered Fairy-Gamalan's family crest on the wing covers? Her crest is a Bluebell over the Moon-Orb. The Bluebell is because she is a Greeter; those fairies whose job it is to welcome the plants as they emerge from their underground sleep. The Moon-Orb is there to show how closely they work with its cycles, just as the plants do."

"Why have you only embroidered a Bluebell? There are many plants that I see being welcomed and tended by the Greeters," asked Scarletina.

"You will learn how each type of plant has its own Greeter; this makes sure that everything is organised; otherwise, you could have Greeters welcoming the same plant and not others. Everyone would be very confused," laughed her mother.

"How do the Greeters know they haven't gone to the same plants, then?" Scarletina asked.

"A good question, little one. Let us use Fairy-Gamalan as an example. When she becomes a Fully-Fledged Fairy, she inherits the family symbol, which is a Bluebell over the Moon-Orb. These symbols are put onto a special stamp made by the Abra. This is used to mark the Bluebells stem once the Greeter has completed the

🍀 *Bess Drew Sherret*

Welcoming Ritual. If the Bumble-Bees see a flower has been missed, which can occasionally happen, due to a late flowering, they report this, and a Greeter will go and sort it out," explained her mother.

"Are the Bumble-Bees the small bees with brown stripes on them that I see flying about in our woodland, Mother?"

"No, they are the Honey-Bees. They are smaller and fly very fast. That is because they have to take the pollen back to their hives where the honey is made. That is their daily mission. Their Queen does not allow them to do anything else, and would be furious if we asked them to work for us! Bumble-Bees are the larger ones with yellow and black markings on them. They fly much slower than the Honey-Bees because whilst they are collecting the pollen, they are also checking that each flower has the fairy symbol on it. As I said, if they notice one has not been welcomed, then they tell the Greeters. Bumble-Bees do not make honey, but keep the pollen for themselves, and for feeding their young. You learn all about the bees, and other life forms, that we share Nightingale Wood with, in the Earth and Moon Circles. So, you see why it is important for you to attend, don't you? Just think of what you will miss learning about if you don't go," said her mother.

Scarletina nodded her head and said, "Yes, I do understand. I have another question I would like to ask.

Can you tell me where theStarDust comes from? I also wonder, how do we get it?"

"This is one of the topics we'll be sharing during the Dark Time of Winter, little one," said her mother, "but we can talk a little about it today as you are clearly interested. The earth is a tiny fragment of the Universe, and there are parts of the Universe that we are unaware of. But we see the stars, don't we, and enjoy how they decorate the night sky?"

"I enjoy looking at them, Mother. They make such pretty patterns, don't they. I love the way they twinkle and shine; it looks like they are winking!" giggled Scarletina.

"Yes, they do, don't they," her mother laughingly agreed, "it's because their light becomes brighter then weaker, almost like us when we breathe in and out. In fact, the Two-Leggeds have names for some of the stars, and enjoy looking at them through something called a telescope. We do not need this tool as we connect with our hearts and feelings, which is how we know when a gift of StarDust is going to be sent."

Scarletina thought about this for a moment then asked, "Where does StarDust come from?"

"Like us, stars live and die; it is the way with all things. When a star dies, its gift to the Universe is itself, and so it becomes StarDust. Some of it floats to other stars and helps to brighten them, and some particles come to earth. We, fairies, get a feeling when this is about to happen. When we do, we ask the Spider-Clan to spin Special Holding Webs, which we spread over the tree tops. When the time comes for the StarDust to arrive, the fairies sit together and we sing our welcome as it floats to earth. We give our thanks to the Star that died for gifting itself to us. When the StarDust settles onto the webs, we take our brushes made of Thistledown, and sweep the StarDust into sacks. These are then stored in The Ancient One, where the King and Queen live, and we know they are safe."

Scarletina asked, "So, if they are stored in The Ancient One, which only a few are allowed to go into, how do we get it from there?"

"Every year the dazzling StarDust Ceremony is held," said her mother, "and sitting on their bejeweled thrones, the King and Queen oversee the collection of the StarDust Entitlement."

"What is ent— that word, Mother, what does that mean?" said Scarletina, stumbling over this new word.

"Entitlement means something we have the right to receive, and that differs with each fairy. During the year, every time we use our StarDust, we have to inform the StarDust Recorder Fairy. She notes how much we used and what we used it for. The Recorder Fairy then bases this information to calculate next year's amount. Some fairies might get less than the previous year, or more. It just depends," her mother explained.

Scarletina's brow was furrowed with tiny thought lines; her mother knew there was a question coming. She also knew what it would be because everyone asked the same question about the entitlement of StarDust.

"How can one fairy be ent…entit…" With a giggle, Scarletina looked to her mother for help.

Her mother smiled back and repeated, "En-ti-tled."

"En-ti-tled, thank you, Mother. How can one fairy be entitled more than another?"

"It all depends on what the StarDust was used for. Let's say it was used to decorate your home. Or perhaps having it spun into clothing for a special occasion. As it was used for your own personal satisfaction, you get the same amount replaced. It is different for someone who has given it as a gift to others, as we have done, using it in the embroidery for Fairy Gamalan's wing covers. Then they receive the amount they have used, plus one handful. It is a reward for using the StarDust in an unselfish way, and for being generous with the gifts of the Universe," her mother said.

"When will I be able to come along to the StarDust Ceremony? I would love to see the King and Queen on their jeweled thrones," asked Scarletina.

"I'm afraid that won't happen until you have your wings, little one. It is a very special, and important, and somewhat long ceremony." Scarletina unsuccessfully tried to stifle a yawn, "Off to bed with you little one;

you looked exhausted. Hopefully, your father will be home tomorrow. You want to be bright-eyed and bushy-tailed, like our Squirrel friends, who are always full of energy, don't you?" said her mother as she tenderly kissed Scarletina goodnight.

"Yes, mother," giggled Scarletina, "I have really missed Father, and it will be so good to have him home again."

Before long, she was lying in her Nestling Place, which is where she slept. Pulling the covers over her, she snuggled down into its softness, and gave a deep sigh of contentment. She was so relieved that her mother knew about the trouble at school. Sleep would come easier, now her conscience was clear.

Leaning her head against Shard, she looked through a crack in its sturdy frame, and saw the stars twinkling at her. Scarletina wondered how long it would be until she was able to feel them, and know when a star died. There was much for her to learn, and to understand. She realised how important it was for her to go to the Earth Circle, to find out about new and interesting things. Learning didn't have to be boring; it could be fun and exciting, too.

Suddenly, she felt a tingling in her head, which seemed to travel down her entire body. With the feeling came the words...

It is I, Suntra-Spider. Well done. I am proud of you. Your thoughts rushed out to meet me, and so I welcomed them in.

I am very pleased with you, Scarletina, and happy that you accept how important it is you attend the Earth Circle. Sleep now, little one."

Could the Spider-Clan hear everyone's thoughts? If they did, Scarletina wondered, wouldn't it be really noisy for them? And when would they get time for their own feelings? Scarletina realised, in future, she would be very careful of what she was thinking, and that was going to be quite a challenge!

Just above Scarletina, Suntra-Spider sat on her web smiling at Scarletina's question about the Spider-Clan being able to read thoughts. Spider-Clan Guardians were allocated to Cropplets because they were able to feel and hear their thoughts. This helped them do their job, which was to watch, protect, and guide their vulnerable Cropplet, who couldn't fly away from any danger. If necessary, they could also talk to them, just as she had done with Scarletina. Their thoughts could only be tapped into whilst they were Cropplets, because once they moved onto the Moon Circle, their thoughts were their own. It didn't do any harm for the little ones to be aware that their thoughts could be heard. Indeed, at times, it was probably a very good deterrent!

Her mother's excited voice called up to her, "Scarletina, Scarletina, come down, Father is home!"

Sleep quickly vanished as Scarletina excitedly leapt out of bed and ran down to greet her Father.

CHAPTER THREE
HUGE SURPRISE

"Father, I am very glad you are home." Scarletina giggled as her father lifted her high above his head, laughing as he twirled her around the room. Her mother looked fondly at the two of them as they finally collapsed onto the chairs, delightfully exhausted with love, and laughter.

"It is very good to be home, too, little one. I have missed you both more than I can say," said her father.

He called out to Scarletina's mother who had gone into the kitchen, "Jasmita, come in here with us. We have things to discuss, do we not?"

"Drewvin, I will be there soon. How about some Raindrop Essence to drink?"

Scarletina was the first to shout out that she would love some, for it was the most delicious tasting drink that Jasmita brewed herself. Her mother collected raindrops from Shard's leaves, and then added secret herbs

 37

and spices and magic words that had been passed down through her family. It was the tradition for mothers to give the recipe to their daughters, once they became Fully-Fledged Fairies. When she drank Raindrop Essence, Scarletina tasted so many different flavours. More than that, it was as if the woodland came to life in her mouth. She loved the sweet, delicate, yet deep flavours, and it was only drunk on special occasions.

Jasmita raised her cup and said, "Welcome back, Drewvin. Now our house becomes a home again. Our family is joined in love and harmony. We are content."

Scarletina and, Jasmita, her mother, and Drewvin, her father, happily joined in the toast. Scarletina's happiness filled her from the top of her head to the tips of her toes, and she felt she might burst with joy. Then, with the suddenness of a bolt of lightning, her joyful mood vanished. Soon her father would ask for the Family Life Journal because he loved to read and talk with them about what they had been up to whilst he had been away. They all enjoyed sharing this time – usually! Today, the prospect of her father reading about her detention at the Circle suddenly made the day less enjoyable, and she trembled at what he might say.

"Before you read our news, Drewvin, I think we ought to give Scarletina a chance to speak. I know she has missed you very much, and perhaps she has some important things to share with you before you begin to read from the Family Life Journal."

Her mother's eyes shone with love, kindness, and encouragement. It was the same look she gave when Scarletina was scared or unsure of herself. Her mother's eyes then looked across the room. Scarletina followed her mother's gaze, and saw her staring at the Family Life Journal, and she understood. She was being given the opportunity to tell her father what had happened at the Earth Circle, before he read about it.

"Thank you, Mother. I would like to do so." With a trembling voice, Scarletina related to her father the events which had led up to her being held in detention. Her tone strengthened as she told her father how she had come to realise the importance of going to the Circle. To misbehave, and rebel, would stop her from becoming a Fully-Fledged Fairy, something she dreamed of. She was determined to show both her parents that she was going to become a better student, to stay out of trouble, and become more responsible.

The room was quiet for what seemed an eternity to Scarletina, with downcast eyes, she stared miserably at the floor. When her father started to speak, she quickly looked up at him, and seeing his serious expression, feared the worst.

"Of course I am disappointed that this thing happened, Scarletina. No parents like to hear that their child has been held in detention, for whatever reason. However, I am pleased that you had the courage to tell me. It shows you are growing up, and leaving the childish Downy stage, and are trying to become a responsible Cropplet. We want to see you carry on in this way, proving to us you are serious about your regrets that this incident happened. I would be a lot unhappier if you had not learnt from this lesson. Now come, and give me a hug."

Scarletina's relief was as big as the happiness she had felt earlier, as her father tenderly embraced her. It certainly made telling the truth worthwhile. Her parents had spoken to her in such a loving and positive way. They had not said it didn't matter, or excused her behaviour. They had let her see the sadness and disappointment they felt about her actions. They were happy that she wanted to become a better student, someone who was determined to prove to her parents that she had learnt an important lesson. Scarletina rushed over to her mother, who tenderly cradled her daughter's face in her hands, kissed both her cheeks and gently whispered, "I am very proud of you, little one. That took a great deal of courage."

"Thank you, Mother. I must always remember to look at your eyes, for you say so much with them."

Her mother sat next to her father, " Now I think it is time for us to share some news with you, little one. Sit down as we need your complete attention."

A puzzled Scarletina did as she was told, but something seemed strange. Both her parents looked odd; they were excited, yet serious at the same time. She couldn't ever remember seeing them like this before, and had mixed feelings, but was mostly fearful. What could the news be? She had a clear conscience because she had confessed earlier, so knew that it wasn't to do with the Circle.

"Your father and I are delighted to say that you are going to have a brother in a few weeks' time," said her mother. Scarletina stared at her parents, who were holding hands, and had the widest smiles she had seen.

"We see you are surprised, little one, but we hope you are happy, too?" asked her father.

"It isn't often we see you at a loss for words. In fact, this must be the first time ever," laughed her mother. But it wasn't her usual laugh, thought Scarletina; it was wobbly, and there were tears in her eyes.

"Where are we going to put it, I mean him. Will he have to share my room?" was all Scarletina could think to ask.

"No, of course not! Shard has already spoken to the Carpenter-Beetles about enlarging our home. They are going to come with the Wish-Fulfiller Fairy to discuss the alterations. Once that is decided, we will all agree on a date for the ceremony. Tell Scarletina about it, Drewvin."

"Shard has agreed to allow us to make our rooms larger, so this means you will still have your own room.

We feel this is very important for you, Scarletina, especially when you graduate to the other Circles. It will be necessary for you to have a quiet place to study, and meditate. To make our home bigger means some of Shard's wood will have to be removed, and this is done by the Carpenter-Beetles. It would be uncomfortable for Shard to have them nibbling away at him, so the Wish-Fulfiller casts a spell, which prevents him from feeling any discomfort."

"Doesn't Shard mind a spell being done, Father?" Scarletina asked.

"No! In fact it would not work if he did not agree to it. We never do a spell that goes against another's wishes or belief; one must always have given agreement for it to be successful," her father responded.

"This is how our fairy clan lives, Scarletina, respecting the ways and feelings of others. We know that by living this way, we create strong bonds of trust with those who share the woodland with us. At the agreed time, the spell is cast, and the Carpenter-Beetles get to work. It doesn't take them long, and they are so tidy, little one. When I was young, my mother had them widen part of the home for her, and I saw for myself how carefully they clean up any mess they might have created. I wish the Two-Leggeds were as tidy in Nightingale Wood; I cannot believe the rubbish they leave around," commented her mother.

"Will you have my brother here, or do you have to go away?" Scarletina asked.

"No, not here, little one. It is something that takes place in the Queen-Beech tree. I will go to the Happening Rooms, and be looked after by the Downy-Greeters. I will have to choose which bower I want to welcome your brother into. Then I will select the herbs and scents that I want to have in the room. I chose lavender and rosemary when I had you, and I still have a sprig of each of them, which the Downy-Greeters saved for me." Scarletina's mother smiled at the memories.

"Why did you choose Lavender? I mean…" Scarletina hesitated. She couldn't put into words what she was feeling because she felt so confused. Her parent's news had shocked her; she had never thought about having a brother!

"Well," her mother responded, "I chose them because I love the gentle, and almost peaceful, colour of Lavender. Rosemary has such a refreshing scent, and it has always helped clear my mind, and it makes me feel calm. With your first born, you have to go to classes where the Wise-Mothers teach you about Fairy-Motherhood, and how to prepare for the coming of your Downy. The Wise-Mothers are special fairies and will be with me when our Downy decides to appear."

"What do you do, Father?" asked a curious Scarletina.

This question made her mother and father laugh. Her father replied, "Not much, compared to your mother! I support, care, and love her in every way that I can, and am there for her, whenever she needs me. Scarletina, you are our precious daughter, and nothing can ever change that. Soon there will be a son to add to our joy! What fun we will have, welcoming him into our family."

Her parents hugged Scarletina, and looked at her with much love and affection. Scarletina realised there was nothing to be worried about. Everything was going to be fine. Different, of course, but now she felt calmer and happier.

"In the Moon Circle," said her mother, "you will learn as I did, the importance of colour and scent. They affect us far more than is sometimes realised. When I was told by the Wise-Mothers you were going to be a girl, I found I was being drawn to the colour of lavender. Though it appears pale, you have to mix three strong colours: red, blue and white, to get it. As for the scent, I have always found the perfume of rosemary to be very uplifting and, also, it is for remembrance. I never wanted to forget one moment of that special and magical time, Scarletina, and I never have." Her mother leant across and kissed Scarletina's forehead, "you are our First-Given, and we look to you to guide your brother in his future life. Will you do that for us, Scarletina?"

"How do the Wise-Mothers know it will be a boy? Do they have feelings about it?" Scarletina asked.

Her mother chuckled, "Yes, they do, and that is all I am going to say about it. They will teach you more about Fairy-Motherhood in the Moon Circle, little one. I am sure we will have more talks about this subject when you do!"

Scarletina sighed and said, "Goodness, there really is such a lot to learn in the Moon Circle, isn't there, Mother. I am glad I will have a special place of my own to study, somewhere that is just mine."

"You know, Scarletina, I think it will be a good idea, whilst the Carpenter-Beetles are making alterations to have them make your room bigger. That way, you can have a study area separate from your Nestling Place. How would you like that?" suggested her father.

"Oh, Father! That would be so amazing! You would do that for me?" Scarletina asked excitedly.

"Of course, little one. We know how much you want to get your wings and become a Fully-Fledged Fairy. This is your Quest, and we want to help you in any way we can," her father replied.

Scarletina clapped her hands with delight, "Thank you! I shall put a sign on the wall saying 'Scarletina's Quest for Fairy Wings.' Well, I suppose my quest has begun, but the sign will be a positive inspiration for me to look at."

"An excellent idea," said her Father, "now let's start thinking about what sort of study you want."

Chapter Four
Unwise Decision

The following morning as Scarletina and Shantreel made their way to school, they talked about the previous day's events.

"I'm glad you didn't get into too much trouble at home, Scarletina. I was thinking about you. Were your parents really mad at you?" asked Shantreel.

"Not really, but the worst part was seeing how upset they were. If they had shouted, and got really mad, I don't think I would have felt so badly. But because they were disappointed in me, I felt as though I had let them, and myself, down. I am going to try to work harder, and not get into so many scrapes. I am the First-Given, and I have to be a good role model for my new brother."

The news stopped Shantreel in her tracks, "What! A new brother! Oh, how wonderful! You must be very excited, Scarletina!"

"I am," said Scarletina, "though, at first I wasn't really sure. But after Mother and Father explained some things to me, I felt a lot better. I think I will enjoy being the eldest."

"Did she tell you about the Happening Rooms in the Queen-Beech tree?" Shantreel whispered.

Scarletina nodded and mumbled, "Not much, though," as she wasn't sure if it was right to discuss such things whilst walking in the wood. Her mother always told her it was important to keep family things private. She had asked if she could share the news with Shantreel, and had been given permission to do so as her family were all Oak-Dwellers.

"You mustn't tell anyone outside of the Oak-Dwellers, Shantreel," Scarletina whispered.

Shantreel made the Oak-Dwellers Vow, "I give the promise of those who dwell within the shelter of the oak." Then Shantreel placed her hands on Scarletina's shoulders, and Scarletina responded by placing her hands on top of her friends, saying "It is with trust and gratitude that I accept your Vow." This ritual was how all Oak-Dwellers made a promise sacred; it was considered a unforgiveable act to ever break that promise.

As they made their way through the woods, they chatted about the topic that was to be discussed at the Earth Circle. "I think it will to be very interesting finding about the clans our fellow Cropplets belong to, and what their family duties are. I mean, there are so many, aren't there, and though we know of them, we really don't know much about them do we?" said Shantreel.

Scarletina nodded her head in agreement, and was just about to reply when she saw her two Ant-Builder friends, who called out, "Greetings of the day to you, Scarletina, and her good friend Shantreel. We wondered if you would like to come and visit our new home? It is now completed, and it would make us very happy for you to see it."

"Greetings of the Morning to you, Ant-Builders. Congratulations on finishing your home; you must all be proud and glad about that." Scarletina responded.

"Yes, we are, especially our Queen. She doesn't like it when there is any disruption in her realm, so she is a lot happier. We hoped that we might see you today so we could extend our invitation. We don't ask everyone, but we trust you, Scarletina," said Ant-Builder A426. Ant-Builder A141 stared hard at Shantreel, who quickly realised the offer was not extended to her, only to her friend.

"I am sure Scarletina would love to visit your new home but, unfortunately, it is a school day and we mustn't be late. We ought to hurry as the bell is sounding, so we do not have much time." Shantreel firmly grasped her friends hand and went to walk away, but Scarletina refused to move.

"I think Scarletina can make her own mind up," argued Ant-Builder A426, "and, to me, she looks as though she wants to come and visit with us. Scarletina is aware that it is a huge honour, and privilege, that many would like to receive."

Scarletina was in a dilemma. She knew she ought to go to school. She had promised her parents that she wouldn't get into any more trouble at the Earth Circle. The Ant-Builders would be disappointed if she refused to visit with them, and it could mean disrespecting their Queen if she didn't go. Oh dear, she thought; there wasn't an easy solution, but she had to make a choice.

"How long do you think we will be? I mean, could I just have a quick look today, and then perhaps, I could visit you another time and stay longer?" suggested Scarletina.

The two Ant-Builders seemed to be considering her suggestion. "Scarletina! It's getting late! We have to leave!" Shantreel whispered urgently, but Scarletina did not answer. "Scarletina! Come on! We can't be late!" Scarletina stubbornly refused to leave. Reluctantly, Shantreel let go of her friend's hand saying, "Sorry, Scarletina, but I am going; you ought to come, too, and if you are late, Tutty-Grandhill will be furious."

"A426 thinks your suggestion, Scarletina, is a splendid idea. Your friend can go onto school on her own. Follow us, and please don't dawdle. We have already wasted too much time today," A141 ordered Scarletina.

"Yes, you go on Shantreel. When Tutty-Grandhill wants to know where I am, tell her what happened. Oh dear, I have to go or they will start getting annoyed with me." With a quick backward glance, and a wave of her hand, Scarletina disappeared into the woods with the Ant-Builders.

"Scarletina Oak-Sharder? Scarletina Oak-Sharder? Does anyone know why Scarletina isn't here? Is she sick?" The piercing gaze of Tutty-Grandhill swept over the Cropplets before coming to rest on a very nervous Shantreel.

Shantreel told the teacher about Scarletina's invitation to see the Ant-Builders' new home. She explained that because it was such an honour, Scarletina had felt obliged to go. Tutty-Grandhill appeared to be carved out of stone; nothing moved, she was perfectly still. Shantreel and the rest of the class held their breath, waiting for the outburst they thought would follow.

"Well, in this instance, Scarletina has made the right decision. To be invited to visit the Ant-Builders' new home is an honour, and one that isn't granted to many. So, to refuse their invitation would certainly have offended them. We know where she is, and who she is with, so all is well. Let us continue with class, and look forward to her return when she can share the details of her visit with us. We will delay talking about our family clans, and their duties until she returns. In the meantime, let us review yesterday's lesson."

Shantreel was relieved that Scarletina wasn't in trouble for her latest escapade. Glancing out towards the path that led to the Circle entrance, she couldn't see any sign of Scarletina. Perhaps it was too soon for her to be returning? But how long would she be with them? Would she be able to find her way back all right? Shantreel didn't know why, but she felt uneasy. She had a nagging feeling in her stomach, or maybe it was her heart? Sighing, she returned her attention to the lesson, before Tutty-Grandhill spotted that her mind was elsewhere.

Scarletina had thoroughly enjoyed her visit to the new home of the Ant-Builders. It was much bigger than she had imagined. In fact, she felt very small beside it. A426 proudly told her that woodland ants were well known for having the largest homes. It wasn't just the size, it was also how creative they were in using pine needles and debris from the woodland floor.

"We extend below ground level, Scarletina," A141 informed her, "you would be amazed if you could see our dwelling from inside, but of course that is not permitted."

"I feel very honoured that you have shown me your home. May I share this with my other Cropplets? I know they will be most interested in hearing all about it." Scarletina asked.

"Of course you may, but you must never give any clue about where it is," was their stern response. Scarletina knew it was very important to the Ant-Builders that the whereabouts of their home remained a secret. To show how seriously she took their request, she did the Winged Oath. She hooked her thumbs together, so her hands made wings, and solemnly promised never to reveal the whereabouts of the Ant-Builders' new home.

Satisfied with this solemn oath, her Ant-Builder friends took her to where a small overgrown path started. "Just continue down that way," A141 said, "and remember, Scarletina, as long as you have the Bluebell Copse on the left side of you, then you are going the right way. This path will lead you to the lane that goes to the Earth Circle. It's easy, Scarletina, but don't go off the main path or you will get lost."

"Thank you both. I must hurry. I really enjoyed my visit," and with a final farewell Scarletina confidently set off.

Chapter Five
Lost and Found

Scarletina began to feel a little anxious. She was unfamiliar with this part of the woodland. In fact, this was the first time she had been here on her own. She scolded herself for being scared. If she kept to the path as she had been told, by the Ant-Builders, all would be well. "And," she said out loud as if to stress her intentions, "I am going to heed their advice!"

She continued walking along the path, constantly looking ahead to see where it went. It appeared quite an easy route, so after a while she began to relax. Her attention drifted, and she thought about her mother, and the Downy brother that would soon be in their lives. She wondered how she would feel when she saw him for the first time? What if he was ugly? She giggled at the idea of this. Then she became very serious; this was her brother!

How could she even think such a thing? He would, of course, be beautiful.

It was whilst her thoughts were busy that she failed to notice she had wandered from the pathway. Not much, but just enough to alter the direction she was going in. The path was easy for the Ant-Builders because they were familiar with it. They were so used to all its twists and turns, they didn't even notice them anymore. When the Ant-Builders reached the left fork, where the old tree stump was, they automatically passed to the right of it. They never gave it a moment's thought because they knew this was the way to go. When they had told Scarletina that the path was easy, it was, from their point of view. They didn't have to pay attention to where they were going. This was not so for Scarletina, who was blissfully unaware that she was now in a place she had never been to before, not even with her parents.

Suddenly Scarletina stopped in her tracks! Where was the Bluebell copse! Spinning round, she looked to her left, and her right, but it was no longer visible! It must be somewhere! Where had it gone? She hadn't left the path, or had she?

Her heart began to beat very fast; she had no idea where she was, no clue which way to turn. Now the woodland seemed less friendly, and fearful tears began to trickle down her face. She felt alone and confused. What was she to do?

"Where am I," she called out, "Is anybody there, can anyone hear me?"

Something was tickling her arm. Looking down, she saw a beautiful butterfly. It was a vibrant deep orange with brown markings across its wings. It was facing her, so she could see its dark eyes, which seemed to be staring at her. Then she noticed its antennae, which seemed to be moving to and fro as its wings gently fanned up and down. It was travelling up and down her arm. She had never seen a butterfly move in such a way before.

"Hello," said Scarletina, "aren't you pretty. What do you want? I feel as though you are trying to talk to me. Are you? I am sorry, but I can't understand you. I wish I could as I am sure you would be able to tell me where I am."

The butterfly flew away from her, and disappeared into a large clump of tall ferns. Scarletina lost sight of it for a few moments, then spotted it, sitting on one of the higher fern leaves, with its wings folded back. It seemed to be waiting. What for, she wondered? How she wished she could understand what it was trying to tell her. The butterfly flew back, and came to rest on her arm, then quickly flew away again, returning to the same leaf.

"What are you trying to say to me? That I should follow you into the tall ferns, is that it?" Scarletina asked. No, that couldn't be right, she thought. It would be impossible to find her way through the thick tall

Bess Drew Sherret

ferns. She couldn't even see the beginnings of a pathway. No, she decided, it would be foolish to try and find a way through.

The butterfly hovered over a fern leaf for a few seconds before it disappeared down into the undergrowth. What was it doing? She saw it appear again, but this time it was much further away.

"I don't know what you are telling me to do! The ferns are too thick. It would be very dark in there. I am too scared to do that, and it frightens me to think that I might get more lost"

The butterfly stayed around Scarletina for a few moments more. Fluttering it's beautiful wings, dipping and circling around her, before finally gently flying away. Scarletina felt more lost than ever. What was she to do? Who would find her? Which way should she go?

Think, Scarletina, think…The worst thing to do is panic. Take some deep breaths, and look around you. Try to see if anything looks familiar.

Scarletina didn't know who was talking and guiding her, but she did as she was told. Standing quite still, she started taking some very deep breaths while she looked around.

Is there something you can climb that might give you a clearer idea of where you are?

Yes! There was. To her right she spotted a tree, whose lower branches she could reach. If she did that, she could climb up, so she could get a higher lookout point. If only she had her wings, she could fly up and be able to see where she needed to go!

Well, you haven't got your wings yet, so climb the tree, Scarletina, scolded the voice.

"Suntra-Spider, is that you?" squealed Scarletina!

Yes, little one. I told you, I am able to receive your thoughts and energies. When you realised you were lost, I was nearly knocked out of my web with your feelings of fear and panic. Scarletina, now you have calmed down. Climb up, and tell me, what can you see?"

Scarletina carefully began to climb the tree, pausing as she did so, to check out what she could see. "I don't believe it! I can see the path that leads to the Earth Circle! I was so close, but never realised." Scarletina shrieked with relief.

Suntra-Spider cautioned Scarletina. *Before you go rushing off, look for signposts that you will be able to recognise and follow. Memorise these as they will help guide you to the path that leads to the Earth Circle. Don't rush, Scarletina, but walk calmly, and look for the signposts. You are already late for school, and by taking your time, you will get you there quicker, more haste, less speed.*

Scarletina made mental notes of the signposts she was to look for. She first saw a twisted tree, which appeared to be dead. She couldn't see any leaves because it was covered in ivy. It even looked as though it might have clumps of black berries hanging from it. Then she noticed a huge boulder that had a very flat top to it, which would make it easy to recognise. On the bend before the lane leading to the school was the Ancient Yew Tree with its white flowers in blossom. How could she not have remembered such an important landmark? She walked past it every day on her way to the Earth Circle!

This was an important lesson; she needed to be more observant, and grateful for the gifts of nature. When Scarletina was satisfied all the signposts were fixed in her memory, she carefully climbed back to the ground.

Suntra-Spider's gentle voice, urged Scarletina to take her time. She also warned her that getting lost again, after being helped by her Guardian, would be viewed very seriously by the Circle Magnificents. They were those rarely seen, but powerful, Heads of Joint Teachings. They were responsible for all of the three Circles: Earth, Moon and Sun. The thought of being brought to the attention of the Circle Magnificents really scared Scarletina. What would her parents say if that happened!

Suntra-Spider knew her words would frighten Scarletina, but she had to know how important it was for her to return to the Circle without any further assistance. In spite of being given very good advice by the Ant-Builders, Scarletina had allowed her mind to wander. This had resulted in all sorts of problems that had placed her in possible danger.

To put herself in the same position again would show that she was not acting in a responsible manner for a Cropplet. This would cause the Circle Magnificents to debate whether she should continue her studies in the Earth Circle. They might decide she needed to wait another season, before continuing her studies, to allow her time to become more accountable for her actions.

"Thank you so much, Suntra-Spider, for coming to help me. I'll make sure I won't have any need to call upon you again today. I promise to concentrate, and not allow myself to get distracted by anything. I will see you after school," promised Scarletina.

Very well, little one. I am going home for a sleep, all this excitement has made me quite tired.

Before leaving, Suntra-Spider watched Scarletina slowly, and carefully, make her way along the path. She was very fond of her charge, in spite of all the scrapes and escapades she got into. In fact, though never admitting this to Scarletina, the spider actually enjoyed being involved in all of them. Scarletina had an inner joy that not every fairy was blessed with, and she radiated a sense of compassion, and care, that was rare in one so young. This made others trust her, just like the Ant-Builders, who were normally extremely secretive and distant. Suntra-Spider would be sorry when it would be time to end the bond they had, but she could still watch her from afar, which gave the spider a lot of comfort.

 Bess Drew Sherret

Scarletina stopped to look at the daffodils. They had been out for some time now. Soon the Daffodil-Farewellers would be preparing them to return to the earth. The daffodils would rest in the shelter of the earth, ready to blossom again next Spring.

She loved their bright yellow trumpet flowers, showing that Winter had gone, and signaling the many joys of Spring. Soon the long days of summer would be here, which meant lots of fun times playing with her friends.

Daffodils seemed very wise to Scarletina. Perhaps it was the way their heads nodded as though they knew everything, as indeed they might. She was looking forward to the Moon Circle for many reasons; learning to talk with the flowers of the woodlands was one of them. Suddenly, she felt something tap her on the shoulder. Spinning round, she saw a furious looking spider that was shaking with anger.

"Who are you and what are you doing here! How dare you interrupt my hunting!" The spider shouted at her.

Scarletina tried to tell him about being lost, but he just carried on yelling at her, "I have been sitting on this leaf since the Giver of SunLight and Warmth awoke, waiting to catch a tasty morsel! This, I would then offer to my lady love, who, if she enjoys my offering, will consent to being my wife. You have no idea of the competition I have to win her affections, you stupid wingless fairy! Because you carelessly wandered, uninvited, into my personal hunting space, you scared away a nice juicy fly. All my patience and diligence has been wasted because of you!"

Scarletina was very scared. The spider seemed mean and nasty, so she said, "I didn't know that this was your own personal…"

"Be quiet! Have you no manners at all? Only speak when I give you permission to, and not before! Because of you, I may now lose my love to another, and my heart will be broken. You will not be surprised that I am very, very angry at your rudeness. You will pay for thoughtlessly invading my home!"

Looking up at him, sitting on a leaf just above her right shoulder, Scarletina realised she had never seen a spider like this before. He was a grey colour, with a yellowish-orange stomach. Even more strange, he appeared to have only four legs! That made him even scarier. Scarletina thought spiders had eight legs, so what was he?

At that precise moment, he moved, and she realised he had been sitting with his two front pair of legs together, and the same with his back legs. That is why it looked as though he only had four legs. He did have eight legs! Scarletina was relieved as this made him an ordinary spider, of sorts. But he wasn't like Suntra-Spider at all, not in looks, and certainly not in manners.

The spider roughly pushed Scarletina away from his leaf, causing her to stumble and fall, "You be careful or my father will report you," said a frightened Scarletina. "He works for the Majesties, and will be most displeased, and angry, when I tell him how you pushed me, and caused me to fall."

The spider leapt from the leaf, and menacingly approached her, his eyes dark, and glittering with anger, "Oh ho, so you are threatening me, now, are you? And do you think I am afraid of your father? No, I am not! I am afraid of no one! Anyway, what makes you think you will see your father again?" he threatened.

As he menacingly moved closer to her, Scarletina backed away, until she could go no further. Her back was pressed against a large boulder; there was nowhere else to go. She was very scared by what he had threatened, and unsure of what to do. If she screamed, would anyone hear her?

He pushed his face close to hers and whispered, "You might make a tasty morsel for my lady love." He brushed her face with one of his front legs, causing Scarletina to shudder, and begin to cry. She daren't run away, or she might get lost again and, anyway, he blocked the path she had to take. Suntra-Spider had gone home to sleep, so she wouldn't be able to feel Scarletina's fear.

"Oh dear, so you are crying now, are you? Don't think your tears will save you from what I have planned for you. You are all alone here, aren't you. There is no-one to help you, ha... ha...ha!" His laughter made her very angry. How dare he treat her like this! What a horrible spider he was, and her anger gave her courage.

"You are very rude, vicious, and unkind. Thankfully, I have never met a spider before that has been so horrible to me. My Spider-Guardian will be very shocked when I tell her about you, how you have abused, and threatened me! I want you to tell me what your name is, unless you are afraid to, because she will want to know who caused me such misery and distress."

"I am happy to give you my name; it is Hackent-Spider, not that it will mean anything to her. We will be from different Spider-clans, and there are many in Nightingale Wood. I am proud to be one of the Nursery-Web clan."

Scarletina started to giggle, "Nursery-Web clan. Oh, my goodness, what a funny name for a spider! Does that mean you have to look after your own baby spiders? Or that you never grow up?"

Scarletina quickly realised her joke was making Hackent-Spider even angrier. She hadn't meant to offend him, so thought she had better apologise, and hope this would calm him down. "Please accept my deepest apologies for my bad manners, Mister Hackent-Spider. You are very fierce, and the name made me giggle, which I also do when I am feeling afraid."

"You have good reason to be scared, let me tell you. I am renowned for my ferocity and skill in hunting. I am

Bess Drew Sherret

as swift as the Wolf-Spiders, and though I may not be able to change my colour, like the Crab-Spiders, I make myself blend in enough to catch food, if I am not interrupted by a stupid wingless..."

Suddenly, he was interrupted by another voice, "But you cannot compete with the Garden-Spiders when it comes to spinning a web, can you, Hackent-Spider!"

"Suntra-Spider!" The relief at seeing her made Scarletina's legs go weak and wobbly, but the fear of Hackent-Spider gave them the enough strength to run to the safety and protection of her Guardian.

"Oh, it is y...y...you Suntra-Spider. It is a long t...t... time since we have seen one another, is it not? May I ask what are you doing here? Do you know this fairy?" he spluttered.

Scarletina was amazed to see the change in Hackent-Spider. The fearsome spider had completely disappeared. Now he was the scared one, stuttering, and looking most uncomfortable.

"I wish I could say it was a pleasure to see you Hackent-Spider, but I can't. I am this fairy's Guardian, and am appalled to find you bullying my charge, in such an aggressive, and spiteful manner. I have no choice but to report you to the Keepers of Peace and Tranquility," was Suntra-Spider's stern response.

"What! No! No, you mustn't do that! I didn't mean any harm! You don't believe I was really going to hurt her, do you? I will admit I lost my temper, a little, and may have said some stupid things. But, I ask you, who could blame me? I was so close to catching the first food of the day, which I was going to present to my lady love. When your 'charge' came blundering along the pathway, uninvited, causing me to lose the fly. It was enough to make anyone..."

Suntra-Spider quickly interrupted, and angrily waved her legs at him, "Bullying of any sort is outrageous, and not to be tolerated. Bullies are without a shred of care, or respect for others. And they always seem to vent their nasty ways upon those who are more gentle, and kind. There is NO EXCUSE for such behaviour. Bullies always act the same when they get found out. It's never their fault, and they unsuccessfully try to hide behind silly and pathetic excuses for their behaviour. Did you feel big and strong frightening this poor Cropplet? You knew she was unable to escape, and you used that power to put her through a terrible experience. You should be very ashamed, Hackent-Spider! I am sure the Keepers of Peace and Tranquility will help you see the error of your ways. Come along, Scarletina. I'll walk with you, to keep you safe, from the unwanted and undeserved attentions of this overbearing and cowardly bully!"

Scarletina felt a little bit sorry for Hackent-Spider as he slowly climbed back onto the leaf; he looked the

Bess Drew Sherret

frightened one now. "What's going to happen to him? Will he get into a lot of trouble?" she asked.

"If I let you in on a little secret, Scarletina, can you promise not to tell anyone?" Suntra-Spider asked.

Scarletina took the Winged Oath; she hooked her two thumbs together, which made her hands look like wings. She placed them against her chest and said, "I promise I won't tell anyone, Suntra-Spider."

"Thank you, Scarletina, for your special oath. Well, the secret is that I won't be informing on Hackent-Spider this time. It's frightening enough for him to have the threat of being reported. He will have a few unpleasant weeks jumping at every noise thinking it will be the Keepers of Peace and Tranquility. I think that'll be a huge lesson for him, and he isn't such a bad spider; it's Springtime and that can make all of us do funny things. Well, not funny. Perhaps more peculiar, and out of character. Perhaps we behave like that because we are so happy that the Dark Time of Winter is over."

Scarletina was glad that Hackent-Spider wasn't going to be reported; she was worried that it might have reflected on her own behaviour again, and said as much to Suntra-Spider.

Suntra-Spider reassured Scarletina by saying, "Goodness, little one, how could you possibly be to blame in any way? You acted very bravely, Scarletina. You have nothing to fear and I am very proud of you. I will accompany you to school to explain to Tutty-Grandhill what happened. Thank goodness that fly landed on my web; I could feel you were in trouble as soon as I woke up."

Scarletina was very relieved, and her heart felt lighter. Suntra-Spider was accompanying her back to the Earth Circle! She didn't have to worry about getting lost again! It was with a happy and grateful heart that she started to look for the signposts she had memorised earlier.

Scarletina realised that Suntra-Spider knew how to get back to the Earth Circle, but she wanted to prove to her Guardian that she had memorised the signposts, so she said, "Suntra-Spider, may I tell you the signposts that I picked out, and then show them to you when we get to them?" Suntra-Spider readily agreed, saying she thought it was an excellent idea.

Scarletina told her Guardian about the butterfly, "I knew it was trying to help, but I couldn't communicate with it. I know what the Ant-Builders are saying, and you, but I couldn't with the butterfly. Why was that?"

Suntra-Spider said the butterfly had realised that Scarletina was unable to understand it. So it tried to demonstrate to her that if she went into the tall ferns, it would guide her. The butterfly would be able to fly above and see where the path was going. It could then return to her, and guide her along it.

"Oh, I see now. Why didn't I think of that? The butterfly must have thought me very stupid."

"No, I don't think so," laughed her Guardian, "you were just very frightened and confused, and that stopped you from being able to understand the butterfly. Normally, you wouldn't have had any problem, but fear takes away our power. You know, you are really going to enjoy learning about communicating to all of our friends in Nightingale Wood."

"Will it be hard to learn how to talk with our friends? I mean, there must be so many different languages: squirrel, rabbit, deer, rook, robin, worm. Then there are the flowers and plants and trees and..."

"Stop worrying about it, Scarletina! You can already talk with many of the creatures in our wood, like the Ant-Builders and the Spider-Clans, can't you. In fact, you are probably the best Cropplet able to do this; not all of them have your ability, you know. Once you are in the Moon Circle, it will all become clearer. You have a gift for talking with our woodland creatures. We can think about the future, but there isn't any point in worrying about it. Usually, when we get there, things are often a lot easier than we thought they would be. Just decide to be a good student, and to listen, and to learn with an open heart and mind."

They had now reached the first signpost, which she pointed out to her Guardian. It was the twisted dead tree, covered in ivy; it was almost impossible to see any branches. There were still some of the small, black berries left on the ivy. They looked very tasty, but Scarletina knew not to eat them, for they were poisonous.

One of the first lessons in the Earth Circle was about recognising poisonous berries. Every Cropplet had been surprised at how delicious they looked. Tutty-Grandhill had explained, that some berries were poisonous only to the fairies, and the Two-Leggeds. These same berries had to look appetizing as they were perfectly alright for some birds and animals. That was why it was extremely important to pay attention to the lesson; they must learn which ones to eat, and which ones to leave alone.

Scarletina's legs were feeling very tired, so she climbed up onto Suntra-Spider's back. It felt so soft and warm that if she hadn't been looking out for the signposts, she could very easily have fallen asleep.

The large boulder was easy for her to recognise, but as they came closer, she noticed some writing on it. Her curiosity was aroused, so she asked Suntra-Spider if the Two-Leggeds had done this. And why they had to mark things with their words? Was it some sort of magic spell?

"Yes, sadly, it was the Two-Leggeds who did this. We do not know why it is done. We have tried to find out, but it remains a mystery to us. There it isn't anything magical about it as nothing ever happens after it is done. Perhaps they think it makes our beautiful, wise, and ancient stone look better? Though, how that could be I have no idea! It seems a very foolish, and pointless thing to do!"

"Is there nothing that can be done to remove it, and return our beloved stone to its natural way of looking?" Scarletina asked sadly.

"Of course there is. The Abra-Elders would have been told about this, and will be preparing a special ointment that will be applied to the writing. This is done when the Moon-Orb is full, and bright. The writings will disappear, then all will be well, until the next time," sighed Suntra-Spider.

"These Two-Leggeds are hard to understand, aren't they?" said Scarletina.

"Yes, indeed, they are," said an obviously sad Suntra-Spider. "But, we can find fairies from other woodlands strange because their way of life is different from ours. We can't blame the Two-Leggeds for not understanding our ways. After all, most of them don't even believe we exist! I just wish they would show more care for our woodland, and behave in a way that shows respect for all who live here."

Finally, they arrived at Scarletina's last signpost, the Ancient Yew Tree, whose branches were filled with white blossoms. Suntra-Spider told Scarletina to get down as they needed to offer their greetings to the Respected-Old-One.

"I offer you Greetings of the Day, Respected-Old-One," repeated a puzzled Scarletina. She quietly asked

Suntra-Spider why were they doing this ritual to the Ancient Yew Tree.

"Because he is the oldest tree in our woodland, explained Suntra-Spider. "No one really knows his age because he always seems to have been here. This is why he is honoured, and why we offer our greetings to him. We do have another Yew tree, but she is deeper into the wood and not as old as he is. You can tell the difference between them both because her flowers are red, and his are white. You will find out more about our beautiful woodland trees when one of the Tree-Keepers comes to give a talk at the Moon Circle."

Scarletina nodded and said, "Yes, I have heard about Tree-Keepers from my parents. When they come to check on the well-being of Shard, I am usually at school. One of my parents is always there to greet them, though. I realised it must be an important visit because they took a day off from work."

"It is very important for them to be there as it shows their respect and care for Shard. After all, he provides shelter and safety for you all, doesn't he? The Tree-Keepers want to make sure that Shard is happy and well, and no harm has come to him." said Suntra-Spider.

"Who would harm our beautiful Shard?" asked Scarletina.

"Sometimes it is nature that causes problems for him. Strong winds can break his branches, which is most uncomfortable for Shard. Sadly, there isn't anything he can do to repair the damage. Worse is when the Two-Leggeds break off branches; we don't know why they do this. They do not use them, but leave them on the ground, under Shard. The Carpenter-Beetles are called in to remove the broken pieces that are still attached, which makes Shard feel happier. The Tree-Keeper also has to check that Oak-Worms aren't attacking Shard. They suck the goodness out of his leaves, which makes him feel very poorly."

"Oh, that sounds dreadful. What can be done for Shard if the Oak-Worms do attack him?" asked Scarletina.

"The Abra organise a leaf picking day. The fairy clans gather, and take off the leaves that are dying. The Abra then say a special spell that protects the oak from any further attacks. When everything is complete, everyone celebrates by having a wonderful picnic beneath the tree."

Scarletina made a vow she would always be on the lookout for Oak-Worms. It really upset her to think about any harm coming to her beloved Shard. As usual Suntra-Spider read her thoughts, "Don't worry about it too much, Scarletina. The Keepers of the Trees are very good at caring for all of our beloved Nightingale Wood. But I think Shard would feel very special if you tell him you are going to make sure nothing hurts him."

Before long, they arrived at the Earth Circle, and could see the Cropplets were listening intently to their teacher. Her fellow students didn't notice their arrival until Tutty-Grandhill stopped talking to offer greetings to Suntra-Spider and Scarletina.

The most relieved Cropplet was Shantreel. She had found it almost impossible not to keep worrying where Scarletina had gotten to. Whilst her teacher seemed quite happy at Scarletina's continued absence, Shantreel didn't share her outlook. She knew how easy it was for her dear friend to get into trouble. She also felt guilty about deserting Scarletina, more worried about being late than supporting her friend.

After the traditional welcome to them both, the teacher said to the class, "Cropplets I am leaving you for a few moments as I need to speak with Suntra-Spider and Scarletina. Please continue with your reading. Stupple-Spider will be staying here to answer any questions you might have. She will, of course, let me know how you have behaved during my absence!" With that, she indicated to Suntra-Spider, and a nervous Scarletina, to go into her private office.

Tutty-Grandhill listened intently as Suntra-Spider related Scarletina's eventful morning. Explaining how Scarletina got lost, and her frightening encounter with Hackent-Spider. "I believe Scarletina has learnt much from this experience," said Suntra-Spider, "and even though she was lost, and very frightened, she took my advice to memorise several signposts. She realised these would enable her to find her way back to the Earth Circle."

"What do you think you have learnt from this morning's events, Scarletina?" Tutty-Grandhill asked her.

Scarletina met her teacher's eyes, "I have learnt, Tutty-Grandhill, to listen, and remember what is being said to me. The Ant-Builders told me to keep Bluebell copse on the left side of me, but I let my thoughts wander; I was day-dreaming. With my mind on other things, I forgot to pay attention to where I was going, and I got horribly lost. I don't know what I would have done without Suntra-Spider's help."

The memory of it all made Scarletina start crying. She had been very brave, but now she was back in the safe surroundings of the Earth Circle, and she couldn't hold back her tears. Tutty-Grandhill comforted her; and said she was glad Scarletina had learnt an important lesson from her frightening time. "Not everyone does. In fact, some never seem to learn. So, the lesson keeps happening to them again and again. Each time getting harder, until they, fortunately, do listen and learn. I accept that you behaved well in the circumstances, Scarletina, so I will not be making a report about this episode. I will speak to all the Cropplets tomorrow morning. They need to understand why no punishment has been given."

Chapter Six
Magical New Friend

Scarletina met with Shantreel at the Place of Decision. Her friend ran up and hugged Scarletina closely, and cried as she apologised for leaving her saying she felt she had let her much loved friend down.

"No, Shantreel, please don't think that way! I am responsible for what happened, not you! I will tell you all about my adventure as we walk to school. It was scary, but Tutty-Grandhill said I have learned a valuable lesson." said Scarletina.

As they strode along Fernshade walk, Shantreel listened in amazement at her friend's escapade. Shantreel said, "Oh, Scarletina, you are so brave! Most Cropplets would have been terrified."

"I was scared, but only realised how frightened I was when Suntra-Spider arrived. I don't want to go through another ordeal like that again," confessed Scarletina.

"What did your parents say?" Shantreel asked.

"They weren't happy that I chose to go with the Ant-Builders. I got quite a lecture from them. They said how silly and dangerous it was to go off into the woods on my own," said Scarletina.

Soon they were sitting at their desks in the Earth Circle, waiting for the teacher to begin calling out the register. When this was completed, Tutty-Grandhill told the class the circumstances that had led to Scarletina's absence. She explained why, on this occasion, she had decided no punishment was to be given. Scarletina had not behaved badly nor without thought for others, and had learnt an important lesson.

"The Ant-Builders' invitation placed Scarletina in a difficult position. I feel, however, you can all learn a lesson from the dilemma she faced. If I had not known why Scarletina was going to be late, then my response today would have been totally different. Fortunately, for Scarletina, Shantreel told me why her friend was going to be late for school."

Scarletina raised her hand to ask a question, " If Shantreel hadn't been with me when the Ant-Builders invited me to their new home, what should I have done? I couldn't refuse them, could I?

Tutty-Grandhill replied, "Had you been unable to let me know you were going to be late, Scarletina, you definitely would have refused their invitation, and arranged another time. You would explain to them that failing to report to the Earth Circle would cause much alarm. That I, your teacher, am responsible for your safety, and well-being. If you failed to come to school, and no excuse for your absence had been received, then your parents would be notified that you were missing. Can you imagine the distress and needless worry they would be put through! I think the Ant-Builders would be happy to suggest another time, after hearing your reasons."

"They looked very upset when I said that I couldn't go with them. I'm not sure they would have liked me to say no." Scarletina replied.

"If they are caring and considerate friends, another time will be arranged, which is good for everyone. You must be careful, Cropplets, not to do something just to please someone else. Especially if it causes problems elsewhere in your life," replied Tutty-Grandhill.

The expression on Scarletina's face said she thought life could be very difficult sometimes! Tutty-Grandhill's eyes went to every Cropplet in the class; they knew this look very well, and it said be silent and pay attention!

"I want you all to listen carefully and understand what I am going to speak to you about." Tutty-Grandhill waited for a few moments, when she had everyone's attention, she said, "If you are unsure whether to do something or not, then don't do it! Your inner voice is urging you to be careful. Repeat after me, WHEN IN DOUBT – DON'T DO IT!"

The students dutifully obeyed, but Tutty-Grandhill thought some were confused, so added, "I want you to remember a time you decided to do something, which felt so right, there weren't any doubts in your mind. Hands up, those who can remember that feeling?"

The Cropplets were hesitant at first, then with growing confidence, the class soon became a sea of upheld hands. "Good, well done. Now, think of a time when you weren't sure whether to do something, but you did it anyway, and things went horribly wrong?" asked Tutty-Grandhill.

Not one hand was raised, so their teacher said, "Come on now, you aren't going to get into trouble. I simply want to see how many this has happened to. Hands up, please."

Scarletina was the first to raise her hand. Then several others slowly put their hands up, too, each sheepishly looking around to see who was owning up to Tutty-Grandhill. "So, only a few of you; that surprises me. Alright, one last chance for anyone to own up." No other student moved, and the ones with their hands held up high were looking very nervous. "I want all of you, who have your hands up, to come out and make a straight line across the room."

Very slowly, and reluctantly, the students made their way to the front of the class. They passed friends, who sat safely in their seats. Some had kindness in their eyes, whilst others seemed to be grinning at them, for stupidly owning up. Quietly, and filled with regret they had owned up, the students faced their seated classmates.

Tutty-Grandhill said to the class, "To the Cropplets who have confessed to making a Mistake, from ignoring their inner voice of caution, I am going to give a Gold Star of Triumph."

Surprised gasps came from everyone in the classroom! A Gold Star of Triumph! Some of the Cropplets muttered to one another saying, how could that be right? It wasn't fair! I thought they would get into trouble! I wish I had gone up now!

Tutty-Grandhill held her hand up to silence the class. "The Gold Stars are being given, in recognition, for the courage these students showed. It is never easy to admit you made a Mistake I am very pleased to see they followed their inner sense of honesty, and though fearing the worst, still took that brave step to own up. Those who did not admit to making bad choices, lacked these Cropplets' bravery.

When it was their turn, each student went on their own to the Gold Star Bush. With an outstretched arm and open hand, they waited for the tree to gift them their award. The Cropplets watched in amazement as the bush became more radiant, and glowed brightly. Every star was bursting with golden light; the bush quivered and shook as it released a Gold Star. It gently floated down, coming to rest on the waiting Cropplets' opened palms.

Holding their precious stars, they walked carefully to Tutty-Grandhill. She gave them the small carved Acorn Cups, in which their stars would proudly be displayed. When the ceremony was finished, the Cropplets showed their excited friends the unexpected reward they had received. Many a student vowed, that next time, they would be brave enough to tell the truth, and admit when they had failed.

With the students back in their seats, Tutty-Grandhill began the next teaching. "As you know, we are going to learn about some of the clans who live in Nightingale Wood. Unfortunately, there won't be time to hear from all of you today. If you aren't called, don't think I have missed you as we will be continuing this on another day. I suggest you make notes, which you can refer to, before you have your final test here in the Earth Circle. To help you with this, I will be handing out to each of you your Personal Quest Diary. This is to be used to record events, special occasions, and your thoughts and experiences. When you finish your Quest, and receive your Diploma, your Diary will be put in the Royal Library archives."

An excited buzz went around the class as the Personal Quest Diaries were handed out. Everyone was very excited to see that on the front cover, written in gold, was their name, the names of their parents, and the name of their clan. Tucked inside the cover was a small pencil with a gold tassel hanging from it. "Oh look! The pencil has our name on it, too," exclaimed one of the students.

Tutty-Grandhill informed the class, "Cropplets, all I want from you today are a few details about your clans. We haven't the time for a lot of information; we just want to give everyone an idea of who you are. So, which Cropplet would like to start telling us about their family?"

Much to Scarletina's surprise, her friend Shantreel stood up, and began to tell the class about her clan. "Our family names are formed by combining the word Oak with the name of the tree we live in. For example, Shard is the name of Scarletina's family's tree so she is called, Scarletina Oak-Sharder. My tree is called Fadd, so I am Shantreel Oak-Fadder. We are blessed to be living within our oak homes as we feel safe and secure in them, and they are part of our family. Oak-Dwellers work for the King and Queen, and there are many positions to fill. My father works for the Circle of Magnificents, who oversee the running of the three Circles for the girls and boys. My mother was a Royal Embroiderer. She has worked on several of the Queen's formal dresses, and is well known for her beautiful embroidery, using StarDust threads woven by the Spider-Spinners."

"What is it like to live inside a tree? Isn't it dark?" asked one of the students.

❀ *Bess Drew Sherret*

"No, because our oak allows us to make small openings in the bark. The opening is covered with double strength webbing, made for us by the Royal Spider-Spinners. This helps keep us cool in the summer, and warm in the winter."

"You say the oak is your family. How can that be?" queried a student.

"The oak surrounds us with its strength, and keeps us safe and warm. It shares itself with us, and it is a great place to play in, too. We feel it's love, and give ours in return. Our families have lived in it for many years; that is why it is part of our family." Shantreel replied.

"What do you want to do when you finally leave the Circles?" asked Abradina.

Shantreel considered the question for a few moments, "I hadn't really thought about that. I do not share my mother's love of embroidery, but I enjoy reading. I would be happy to work in the Royal Library. It is very large, and holds the records of every fairy that has lived in Nightingale Wood, and the names of the Kings and Queens, too."

"Thank you, Shantreel. That was very good. Now we will move onto someone else. Would you like to go next, Abradina? I'm sure everyone would like to hear about your clan." suggested Tutty-Grandhill.

Scarletina was excited. Abradina had agreed to talk about her clan! No one knew much about the Abra, for they were the Seekers of Magic, always secretive and mysterious. Scarletina thought Abradina was very mystical. Her dresses were always of deep blue, with hints of purple and silver that seemed to sparkle in the sun. She wove unusual leaves and flowers into her long dark hair. Every other Cropplet's tunic had to be in shades of green; only the Abra were allowed to wear different colours. Their cloth was different, too, so you always knew who was a member of that magical clan.

Her twin brother, Abragan, looked just like her, but with short curly fair hair. He got into a lot more mischief than his sister. The Abra were the only clan ever to have twins; this made them seem even more unusual and magical to their classmates.

The brother and sister enjoyed being together in the Earth Circle, it was a very happy time for them. Once their wings sprouted, and they graduated, Abragan would go to the Star Circle, and Abradina to the Moon Circle. The both hoped they would come together again in the Sun Circle, but it would depend on when they would graduate.

"My family live in the place known as Magicana," said Abradina, "only those of the Abra clan know where Magicana is. Magicana's exact position in Nightingale Wood is a well-kept secret. Every member of the clan is sworn to secrecy. If an Abra tried to reveal where Magicana is to someone outside of our clan, their words

🍀   *Bess Drew Sherret*

would not be heard. Their voices would be magically silenced, and a purple mark would appear on their cheek. Everyone would know they tried to betray our secret place; that is the magic and power of the Abra. We are the connection to the seen and unseen. We are the link between our fairy hearts and those of our woodland companions. We talk with the Spiders, snakes, squirrels, rabbits, the frogs and fish, trees, flowers and plants. We are able to unite with all living creatures here in Nightingale Wood. We train as you do, in the Three Circles, but also take magic studies and learn the teachings of the Abra."

All the students seemed spellbound whilst Abradina was talking. Her voice had a soothing, hypnotic sound to it. When she stopped speaking, they struggled to get their attention back into the classroom.

"Thank you for some very interesting insights into your clan, Abradina. Has anyone any questions?" said Tutty-Grandhill.

"Yes, Scarletina, what is it you would like to ask," prompted Tutty-Grandhill.

"I have noticed that you do not remain with the rest of us when we have our break-times; where do you go? I am sorry, I do not wish to appear rude by asking but…"

"We don't mean to seem unfriendly, Scarletina," Abradina quickly replied, "but Abra's are Sensitive's, which means we feel the emotions of those around us.

As my brother and I are still learning to control this, it can be quite exhausting for us. We become invisible, to give us time re-energise ourselves, and come back to class refreshed."

"Does that mean when you are invisible that you could be sitting with us, and hear what we are saying?" asked Darbetta of the Keepers of the Waters Clan.

"We could, but we do not. It is forbidden to use our mystical talents in any way that might hurt, or offend another. We go away from you all, to a quiet place, and always come back into physical form when we return," Abradina reassured her.

"Can you stop being a Sensitive?" asked a curious Scarletina.

"No, we do not have a choice as it is something we are all born with. There are those who go on to develop this skill, to a higher degree. Whilst others seek to connect more deeply with our fellow creatures. Only a few are selected by the Mystics to study magical skills."

Scarletina could have continued asking Abradina questions, but Tutty-Grandhill chose to move onto one more person, "Darbetta, tell us about the Darbs, the Keepers of the Waters."

Scarletina was thrilled that someone like the shy and timid Darbetta was being asked to speak about her clan. "We of the Darbs are entrusted to look after our streams and ponds, to make sure the waters are kept crystal clear, so they sparkle in the rays of the Giver of SunLight and Warmth. By keeping the water clean, the frogs and newts, otters and fish, Dragon-Flies, plants and many more, are nurtured and kept safe. We of the Darbs are the only clan as happy under the water as on the land. We are blessed to share the secrets of the waterways and to enjoy their bounty and delights. We ride with the Dragon-Flies, and watch with them as the young ones emerge from under the water to dry their wings before taking flight. Tending the tadpoles is always fun because they wriggle a lot, and can be hard to get hold of," giggled Darbetta.

Shantreel whispered to Scarletina that she had never heard Darbetta speak for so long, or with such passion. "Would you like to share your whispered words with us, Shantreel?" Tutty-Grandhill asked.

Shantreel's face turned a deep shade of red; she looked at her teacher and stuttered, "I...I said that I hadn't heard Darbetta talk for that long, or with such feeling before. I mean... Oh dear. I wasn't being horrible, Darbetta. It was really lovely to hear you talking about your clan...I mean..." Shantreel's voice was quivering with unshed tears.

"Shantreel, it is never good manners to whisper about someone else. It matters not whether you are saying something nice, or horrible. I understand you were surprised at how expressive Darbetta was, but it is bad manners to whisper whilst someone is speaking. I do not want to hear anyone doing this again. Well done, Darbetta. Take this whispered compliment from Shantreel, and share it with your family; they will be very proud of you."

Darbetta came over to Shantreel during a break and said, "Thank you for saying those kind words about me, and I know you wouldn't have said anything horrible or nasty. You are so gentle and generous to everyone. I cannot imagine you ever being unkind. I felt very sorry for you when Tutty-Grandhill reprimanded you."

"Oh, Darbetta, thank you for saying that. It really was fascinating listening to you. It must be such fun being able to swim with the creatures that live in the waters. I love sitting by the stream, and trying to see the life that lives there. I have to make sure I am well hidden because if I am seen, everything disappears very quickly. The problem is, when I am hidden, it makes it hard to see everything clearly."

"Perhaps you would like to come with me one day, and I can introduce you to some of my friends who share our waters. Oswaldo, the otter, is such fun, and tells amazing stories. Of course the frogs are very happy when we visit with them; we usually end up have a sing song," giggled Darbetta.

"I would love to do that Darbetta, and how kind of you to offer. I shall have to ask my parents for their permission, of course, but I don't think they will say no!"

"And, I would enjoy showing you around. There is a lovely flat stone by the Playful Pond where we could have a picnic. My family and I go there a lot, and we always have so much fun."

"Why is it called the Playful Pond?" Shantreel giggled.

"It is known by that name because that is where all the young tadpoles are hatched, and everyone has such fun playing with them."

Scarletina felt a slight pang of jealousy as she heard her best friend Shantreel making plans with Darbetta. She felt left out. Shantreel hadn't called her over to join in with their plans; how mean was that! A gentle voice whispered, *Remember, friendship doesn't mean you own someone, or that they can only be friends with you. The true bond of friendship is always a gift to be shared.*

Scarletina realised it was Suntra-Spider who was speaking these wise words to her. Of course it was silly and childish of her to get jealous. It was just different seeing Shantreel with someone else. Later, she would happily join in with Shantreel's excitement about her visit to Darbetta's home.

"Are you all right?" Scarletina turned, and met the concerned green eyes of Abradina.

" Yes, thank you. Why do you ask?" said Scarletina.

"You looked a bit sad, and angry, for a moment. That was all. I was worried," Abradina confessed.

"Thank you for asking. I didn't realise my thoughts showed, but maybe they do to you, being a Sensitive?" Scarletina asked.

"Yes, it allows us to see a lot more than others do. It is a blessing, but can be quite draining sometimes," Abradina responded with a gentle smile.

"My Guardian, Suntra-Spider, is good at letting me hear her thoughts. She is very wise and gives me guidance. A few moments ago, she helped me realise my thoughts were silly and unkind."

"Yes, I know that Cropplets have a Guardian whilst they are in the Earth Circle. We are given an Abra Guardian. It is felt that we have to learn to use our…let's say gifts, without help from anyone, other than the Abra, of course."

"It must be hard for you," said Scarletina. "I mean, are you allowed to have friends outside of the Abra clan?"

Abradina shrugged her shoulders, "I'm not sure as no-one outside of the Abra have ever asked to be my friend. You see my brother, Abragan, and I, are always together. Perhaps we seem happy enough being with one another, and that is why no one else has tried to become friends with us."

"No, it's not that. I think it's because you are from the mysterious and magical Abra clan. It makes us a little bit scared of you, which is why it was great to hear you talk about yourself, and your clan today," said Scarletina.

"It isn't easy for us being different from the other Cropplets. I am surprised, though, to find out you have been scared of us. I think finding out about each other, and our clans, is going to make it easier for everyone become friends," suggested Abradina.

"I have really enjoyed talking with you, Abradina. Perhaps we could do it again?" asked Scarletina.

Abradina nodded and said, "I would like that, but you're sure you aren't asking me because Shantreel is beginning a friendship with Darbetta?"

Scarletina blushed to the roots of her hair, "Gosh, it is going to be difficult having you for a friend. You're like Suntra-Spider; you can read my thoughts, too!"

Abradina took hold of Scarletina's hand, "No, I'm not allowed to do that. Abra's are trained to be watchful, and alert, to what is going on around them. I saw you watching Shantreel with Darbetta, and heard them making plans to meet. You looked upset. It doesn't mean she has stopped liking you. We want to get to know one another, but that won't stop you having Shantreel as your friend, will it?"

Scarletina gave an embarrassed laugh, "Of course not! I have always wanted to get to know you, Abradina, but never had the chance before."

"Scarletina, you had better hurry up as Suntra-Spider will be waiting for you," called Shantreel.

" Yes, I'm coming," called Scarletina, "I had better go, Abradina. Thank you for our chat. I think we are going to be good friends."

Chapter Seven
Making Amends

"So, did you have an interesting time today, Scarletina?" asked her mother as they cleared away the dinner things.

" Yes, I did. I enjoyed hearing about the clans that share out woodland. Especially about Abradina, though she didn't say much about the Abra clan. At least we got the chance to talk to each other, which was really great. I hope we can become good friends, and Shantreel is going to visit Darbetta. It's strange, we have been in the same class all this time, yet have never chatted to either of them before today."

"And why is that, do you think?" asked her mother.

"I suppose the Cropplets have remained within their own clans. We seem to have stayed with the people we are familiar with," Scarletina responded.

"That is why Tutty-Grandhill has days like today," said her mother, "it is important to find out about the lives and ways of others. It helps us to understand them better, which makes our lives easier and happier. Look how much fun you have had, learning about some of the other Cropplets in your class. New friends have been made because you found out how nice they are."

"I didn't always feel good today, Mother," Scarletina admitted.

"Really, why was that Scarletina?" her mother asked.

"I am sorry to say that I got jealous when I saw Shantreel with Darbetta. I could see how they liked one another, and they were laughing and chatting, and I felt left out and" Scarletina hesitated to put her feelings into words.

"And?" asked her mother.

Scarletina looked at her mother and saw that special smile, encouraging her to be open and honest.

"And I felt angry that she could forget me so quickly, and become friends with a Cropplet from a different clan. Then I heard Suntra-Spider's voice, and she told me true friendship is about sharing, not owning someone. Later Abradina came over because she thought I was upset, and we started talking, and I liked her straight away. What a coincidence; Shantreel and I find new friends at the same time!" laughed Scarletina.

Her mother gave her a big hug, "I am very proud of you, little one. Today, you learnt an important lesson. Letting go of bad feelings that can only harm you. It happens to everyone, young and old alike. The Universe offers such times to help us grow, and to become more thoughtful and caring about ourselves, and then others."

"Shouldn't we put others first, Mother?" questioned Scarletina.

"It's not about putting others first, or last. It's simply, that we are responsible for who we are. If we think too much about others, then we can fail to work on ourselves. Then we don't refine and polish our own personal qualities, and fulfill our destiny. When you experienced the bad energy of jealousy, what might those angry feelings have made you do?" her mother gently asked.

Scarletina thought for a few moments and replied, "I think I could have quarreled with Shantreel, and I might have said some unkind things to her."

" Yes, and your friend would have been hurt, and troubled, but who do you think would have been more upset, you or Shantreel?"

Scarletina quickly replied, "I think I would have been, Mother."

"And why would you have been unhappier than Shantreel," coaxed her mother.

"Because it was me who started it, and I would have felt really awful for saying such hurtful, and mean things to my friend," confessed Scarletina.

"Exactly," said her mother, "but, you stopped those bad feelings. You took control, and didn't do something you would be sorry for. That is what is important, Scarletina, recognising, and not giving in to those types of harmful thoughts. It will always make you stronger."

"Thank you, Mother. Gosh, life can be hard sometimes, can't it? I am glad I didn't argue with Shantreel as she is very special to me. May I go and see her as I want to talk with her, before its time for bed?" asked a subdued Scarletina.

"Of course, but don't be too long," cautioned her mother, "and stay on the branches. Don't go down to earth level. It's the time of night when the Two-Leggeds come out to walk."

Scarletina safely arrived at her friend's home, and before long was sharing Shantreel's Nestling Place. Scarletina told her friend, honestly and openly, about her jealous feelings.

Scarletina finished by saying, "I'm not proud of how I felt Shantreel, and it was important that you know."

Shantreel hugged her friend close, "Scarletina, one of the things I love about you is your honesty. Thank you for telling me, but I have to confess, we are the same! I felt a little jealous and left out when I saw you with Abradina!"

This confession sent them into screams of laughter, with promises never to feel that way again. They knew how much they cared about each other, and how silly they had been. It was going to be fun hearing about each other's new adventures.

"Have any asked about visiting with Darbetta yet?" Scarletina asked.

"Yes," responded Shantreel, "my parents have agreed. Next week, we will go to meet Darbetta's family. I am so looking forward to it. Are you going to visit with Abradina?"

"My mother is happy for me to be friends with Abradina," Scarletina said, "but as for visiting her? I don't think that will be possible. Remember, she said that only those of the Abra clan know where they live. I suppose she could come to my home, or maybe we could meet somewhere else? I think we will have lots to tell each other, about our new friends, don't you? Anyway, I had better go back as I promised mother that I wouldn't be long. I'm so glad we had this talk. See you tomorrow at our usual place, Shantreel."

When she arrived home, Scarletina was thrilled to see her father was there. She was often in bed when he got back from work. Running up to him, she giggled as he lifted her high into the air. He kissed her on her cheeks saying, "Hello, little one, you have been making new friends I hear?"

"Yes, it's very exciting," said Scarletina, "I have always wanted to get to know more about the Abra."

Scarletina caught a look between her father and her mother, "Yes, and we need to talk to you about that Scarletina. Come sit by me," said her father.

"We are pleased that you are making new friends in the Earth Circle," said her father, "but you must understand that to be friends with someone of the Abra clan can cause problems."

"Why?" asked a puzzled Scarletina, "I mean, all we want is to meet and have fun, just like Shantreel and I do."

"The Abra clan, for obvious reasons, keeps themselves apart from all others in Nightingale Wood. Though all fairies are capable of minor magic, only the Abra train to become Mystic Masters. Magic is the Abra's way of life, and it is a secret life. They do not welcome anyone from the outside. You must never go anywhere, or do anything, with Abradina, that might bring you into contact with any Fully-Fledged Abra fairies. Do you understand me, Scarletina? This is a very serious matter," her father warned.

"Yes, I do understand. Abradina told us that fairies get a purple mark on their cheek, if they reveal where the Abra clan live. But we will be able to meet, won't we, Father?" pleaded Scarletina.

"I'm not promising anything Scarletina. We will have to see. I need to find out more about it all. We don't

Bess Drew Sherret

want you getting into any trouble!" Her father changed the topic, showing Scarletina that the discussion about Abradina was closed. "Now, your brother will be arriving soon, and we wanted to tell you what happens when he does. I think it's best if your mother explains everything to you."

Scarletina's mother explained, "Your brother is nearing readiness, snuggled inside the Birthing Cocoon, which is protected in the Happening Room. It has been decorated with the chosen woodland flowers, and herbs. The Cocoon is guarded, and protected by four Dragon-Flies at all times. This is necessary because many years ago, the Blackdown Wood fairy commune tried to steal some of our newly born Downies. The fairies of Blackdown Wood, who sadly, have lost their faith in the power of good, may try again so..."

"Why did they try to steal our Downies? Didn't they have any of their own?" interrupted Scarletina.

"No, they didn't," said her mother. "You see, believing in the power of good makes fairies strong, and their magic more powerful. Because the Blackdown Wood fairies lost their faith, their magic became weaker and weaker. Their Magic Skills faded, until it made it impossible for them to have their own Downies."

"What happened to them, the fairies that stopped believing in the power of good?" Scarletina whispered.

"You will learn all about this when you reach the Moon Circle, Scarletina. It is not for you to hear yet. You're not ready to understand such things. All you have to know is that your brother is loved and protected at all times. The Downy-Greeters will send for me to welcome his arrival. Special magic is performed by one of the Mystic Masters; it is a very happy and joy filled time. When the ceremony is finished, you and your father enter the bower and, together, we welcome and bring home your brother."

"The answer is no, Scarletina! I know you want to ask more about the Blackdown fairies. All will be explained to you, at the proper time, in the Moon Circle. I do not want to hear any more about it," said her father in his, don't question me voice!

"Right off to bed with you, little on. You can hardly keep your eyes open. Come, kiss us goodnight," said her mother.

Scarletina did as she was asked, and kissed both parents, before climbing into her Nestling Room. She lay on her Nestling Place, soft with dried grass and herbs, but tonight she did not notice their fragrant scent. She felt quite cross, and disappointed, that her parents wouldn't tell her more about the bad fairies of Blackdown Wood. Still, she consoled herself. It might soon be time to go to the Moon Circle. Though, of course, she had to wait until her wings sprouted before this could happen.

Bess Drew Sherret

There were some Cropplets who had been in the Earth Circle for ages, even before she started. Her mother had told her, they obviously hadn't learnt all the lessons. They would remain in the Earth Circle until they had completed every lesson and teaching; they had to. No one could cheat, and pretend they knew something. The Circle of Magnificents always knew the right time that a Cropplet's wings would sprout, and then graduate to the Moon Circle.

Scarletina looked at her reflection to see if there was any sign of her wings. Disappointingly, nothing showed. Then the soft voice of her Guardian said, *Patience, Scarletina. You have no control over your future. Your wings will form when you are ready, and not before. Concentrate on the present. Enjoy your time in the Earth Circle. You cannot hasten your move to the Moon circle. Patience is a hard lesson, but one that must be learnt.*

Dear Suntra-Spider, always giving such wise advice, thought Scarletina. She yawned, and began to wonder what might happen tomorrow. Then she giggled. Oh dear, here she was thinking about the future again! Tucking down under the covers, she dismissed any thoughts about the following day, and promptly fell asleep.

Chapter Eight
Scary Moments

The last lesson of the day was over at the Earth Circle, and Scarletina and Shantreel were starting their walk home, when Shantreel said, "Isn't that your father waiting at the Ancient One tree, Scarletina?"

Racing up to her father, Scarletina asked, "Why are you here to meet me? Is anything wrong?"

Her father gave a huge grin and said, "No, little one, quite the opposite. It seems the Downy-Greeters think your brother is ready to be welcomed, so your mother is there, and we are going to join her." Holding her father's hand, they set off towards the Queen-Beech tree.

Scarletina was very excited. It was time; her brother would soon be here. Suddenly, she felt uneasy. There was a nagging feeling in the pit of her stomach. She tried to ignore it, but it wouldn't go away. If only she could ask Suntra-Spider for her advice. When she was with her family, Suntra-Spider wasn't allowed to connect with her. That was the rule for all Guardians.

Scarletina felt there was a threat to her brother, that he was in some kind of danger! Why should he be? He was protected by the four Dragon-Flies, her mother, and the Downy-Greeters. Why was she feeling so anxious?

"You are very quiet," commented her father.

Scarletina was unsure what to do. Her father would probably think her silly, if she spoke of her fears. He might even get cross with her. Today was a very special time for her family, so she replied, "I'm fine, just thinking about my brother."

When they reached the Queen-Beech tree, her father said they had a special ritual to do. He told Scarletina to lay the palm of her hand on the Queen-Beech tree trunk. He did the same saying, "We thank you for protecting our young, and for giving them a place of safety and security. We show our gratitude by offering you this StarDust."

Her father took a small packet out of his pocket and said, "Scarletina hold out your other palm, and I will put some StarDust into it. I want you to carefully place pinches of the StarDust onto the Queen-Beech's trunk, and gently rub it along the bark. Can you do that for me?"

"Yes, Father, but won't some fall onto the ground?" asked Scarletina.

"Of course, but the Queen-Beech tree lives above and below the ground; this way, all of her will receive our gift," he explained.

Scarletina carefully took a pinch of StarDust, and then gently rubbed it onto the rough bark. It stayed there for a few seconds before vanishing into the tree. Looking down at the ground, she watched the fallen StarDust gradually disappear into the earth until not a trace was left.

Once their task was completed, and the Queen-Beech tree had accepted their offering, they entered the Holding Room. This is where families greeted the New Arrivals. It was lit by dancing Fire-Flies that flitted between the draped, coloured threads spun by the Spider-Spinners. Orange Lady-Birds led them to some cushioned seats, where they were told to wait.

Once seated, Scarletina began to relax, and felt that there wasn't any need for her to be worried. Everything looked warm, cosy, and safe. Then she noticed her mother talking to the Dragon-Flies, they didn't seem happy at all. In fact, they all looked very worried, indeed.

"Stay here for a moment, Scarletina," said her father. "I am going to see your mother to make sure everything is ready for us to greet your brother."

She watched as her parents talked with the Dragon-Flies, and she could see something wasn't right. Both of them had their very serious faces on, and the last time she had seen them look like that was when a fire had blazed through the woods, and had threatened Shard.

She wondered what could be making them look so troubled? The answer came to her in an instant! Of course! The Blackdown Wood fairies!

Her parents looked fearful because they knew the Blackdown Wood fairies were planning a raid. That had to be the reason, thought Scarletina!

Nervously, she looked around the Holding Room, half expecting to see the wicked fairies creeping around the room preparing to attack! Shadows seemed to be lurking in every corner as though waiting to pounce. What was that noise!

Scarletina's heart was beating so loudly; she thought it would stop her hearing anything else. She was sure she could hear whisperings, and muttering, but from where? She listened more carefully; it sounded as though it came from outside. Probably they were checking things out, before charging into the Holding Room!

Slowly, Scarletina began to creep towards the entrance. It was necessary for her to look outside to see what they were up to. Once she knew for sure where the bad fairies were, she would shout out the Warning for Extreme Danger! Every fairy knew the danger call, AWARE! AWARE! AWARE! As soon as the Dragon-Flies heard that cry, they would begin to defend, and protect the Queen-Beech tree, and the Downies would be safe.

It was menacingly dark outside. All around her the leaves moved suspiciously, and ominously rustled. It had to be them, thought Scarletina! Goodness, she was scared. Urging herself to be brave, she braced herself to leave the protection of the Queen-Beech tree. Gathering her courage, she tiptoed to the entrance. Holding on to the tree, she leant out as far as she could, without giving herself away, and peered into the blackness.

What was that! Something moved on the branch above her. She strained her eyes trying to see what it was. If only she had her wings, she would have been able to fly up there and see. There it was again! Now all was quiet. Where had it gone! She could feel something was out there. What should she do?

When her father touched Scarletina's shoulder, she leapt so high in the air, it seemed she did have wings. The spine-chilling scream that came out of her mouth echoed around the Queen-Beech tree waking the sleeping Downies, the dozing mothers, and causing much alarm!

Her father was shocked to see Scarletina's reaction. "Little one, whatever is the matter? Why did you jump and scream like that?"

The shock made Scarletina forget about making her father cross! So she told him of her fears and anxiety, how she had seen her parents looking very worried, and talking to the Dragon-Flies. Putting these thoughts

Bess Drew Sherret

together made her believe that the Blackdown fairies were planning another raid.

Her father hid his smile from Scarletina. It would have been most unkind to have laughed at her fears. He could see that she had been very scared, "Scarletina, tell me. What were you going to do if you found the Blackdown fairies outside the entrance?"

"I didn't really have a plan, Father," Scarletina confided. " I thought I heard whisperings, and it sounded as though they were coming from outside. If I saw the Blackdown fairies, then I could give the Warning for Extreme Danger, AWARE! AWARE! AWARE!"

Her father hugged Scarletina and said, "I am very proud of you, little one. You showed great courage, but it's not the Blackdown Wood fairies that is worrying us. The Spider-Clan have warned that the Two-Leggeds are going to come here tonight, and have a party. It is worrying if they have a fire in our precious woods, especially so close to our beloved Queen-Beech tree. There is nothing for you to worry about, Scarletina, because the Abra are involved. They can use their magic to help, if it becomes necessary."

Tears of relief fell from Scarletina's eyes. She was glad to have told her father about her fears, and very happy that she had made him proud of her. "Come on," said her father with a smile, "it's time we said hello to your brother."

Scarletina would never forget the first time she saw him. "He is so tiny, Mother. Hasn't he got a lot of hair! Did I have that much hair? Has he been named?"

Her mother smiled at Scarletina's questions, and replied. "Yes, he is tiny. Yes, you had as much hair. And yes, the Downy-Greeters consulted with the Abra, and they have given him the name of Jagon. Do you like it, Scarletina?"

"Yes, I do," agreed Scarletina, "it sounds a strong name. Even if it is shortened to Jag, it still has a lovely sound to it. When will you be bringing him home?"

"We are going to come now!" laughed her mother, "All is well with him, and I am anxious to be home, and safe within Shard, our strong oak. Before we leave, we must go and give our thanks, and gratitude, to the Downy-Greeters."

Chapter Nine
A Sad Day

After such an exhausting and exciting day, Scarletina was relieved to be lying in her Nestling Place. She could hear the Two-Leggeds shouting and laughing, they made so much noise. Why was that? Thankfully, they didn't often come into this part of the woodland at night, but kept to the outer edges. It was said they were scared to be in the thickest part, where it was always darker, especially when the Moon-Orb was not seen. So why had they come here this time?

Scarletina prayed they would not harm the woodland, but it was then she smelt wood smoke. Carefully, she climbed out onto the branches, and through the trees, she could see a fire glowing. It was very close to their beloved Queen-Beech tree.

The Two-Leggeds were getting noisier, screaming and laughing. Why do they have to do that? Didn't they know night-time should be quiet? With that clamour, how could Sleep be able to come to everyone?

Suddenly, the screams changed, and the laughter wasn't there. The shouts sounded very different, not happy at all! Scarletina couldn't see anything to cause this. Then, coming through the trees, she saw a thick yellow swirling Mist. Where had that come from? This wasn't the time of year for such weather? The Mist moved quickly and formed strange shapes and sounds.

Scarletina had never seen or heard anything like this before. The Two-Leggeds were yelling out to one another, sounding confused and lost.

The Mist became thicker and seemed to grow as tall as the trees, and the strange, haunting noises grew even louder. The Two-Leggeds sounded as scared as she had been when she thought the Blackdown fairies were outside the Queen-Beech tree. What were they be afraid of? It could only be the Mist and the sounds, but why would that frighten them so much? What could they see that she couldn't?

The Mist suddenly disappeared, and so did the noises. Scarletina couldn't see the fire burning brightly anymore, it seemed very dark now. The Two-Leggeds weren't shouting or running around; they were speaking very quietly, and it sounded like they were leaving!

Scarletina sat on the branch for a while longer, waiting for the woodland to return to its quiet night-time hum.

Bess Drew Sherret

When it did, she knew it was safe to go to bed. Peace had been restored to Nightingale Wood. The Abra must have brought in the Mist, and eerie sounds with Magic, but why had it made the Two-Leggeds leave? What had they seen in the shapes that she hadn't? She wondered if she would ever find out...

Scarletina was awoken by the sound of wailing, and deeply mournful sobbing. It frightened her. Whatever was the matter? Had something happened to the Queen Beech tree? Her stomach turned over at the thought of this. But why else would the fairies be in such distress?

Her mother called out in a voice that had to be obeyed, "Scarletina, get dressed as quickly as you can. We have been called to Bluebell copse. Don't ask any questions. Just get ready."

Scarletina dressed quickly, and was soon walking with her mother towards Bluebell copse.

"Do not ask me any questions, Scarletina. I am as much in the dark as you are. I fear it can't be anything good, by the melancholy that envelopes the wood today," her mother said sadly.

When they arrived at Bluebell copse, Scarletina's eyes filled with tears when she saw dozens of Bluebells lying twisted and broken. They had been pulled from the earth, and cruelly cast aside. Who could have done that?

The Bluebell-Greeters and Bluebell-Farwellers sobbed their grief. They tenderly lifted the dying plants, and held the bruised, limp, and lifeless leaves to their cheeks, all seeking to comfort the dying plants.

Scarletina cried out, "Mother, what has happened? Who hurt the Bluebells?"

She had never seem her mother look so sad. "Scarletina, a Keeper of Peace and Tranquility is going to speak about this. Listen to his words for this is a terrible day in Nightingale Wood."

A hush fell over the woods. The birds stayed silent. Squirrels ceased to scamper and chatter. The spiders stopped spinning. All of the woodlands joined together, waiting, and grieving.

The Keeper of Peace and Tranquility began to speak. "Today, our hearts reach out to the Bluebell clan. They have the unhappy task of returning to the earth some of their Bluebells. We are all aware of the joy and delight these flowers give to so many with their beauty and perfume. They seek only to give pleasure and ask to be left unharmed, to grow and blossom, before returning to the Earth.

Sadly, last night, a few of the Two-Leggeds chose to tear our beloved plants from the earth and throw them aside. It did not occur to them that, by doing this thoughtless and cruel act, they were killing something of beauty. Not all of them did this dreadful act; some even tried to stop them, and to them, we send our thanks and blessings. Because of them, most of our beautiful Bluebells were saved from destruction.

We cannot understand their actions. What happiness could they have felt when they carelessly ripped out our flowers, then threw them away? To us, all life is special, and to be respected and treasured. We are all part of this world, and surely, if we harm another, we cannot help but harm ourselves.

The Abra clan used Magic to put out the Two-Leggeds' fire. They brought in the Mist, which scared them, and made them leave before any further harm was done. We knew they would run away from the Mist for they are often afraid of things they do not understand.

We must not blame all the Two-Leggeds. Many of them try very hard to help us; they work to ensure our woodlands remain safe from many dangers. It is at times like this, that we must remember the positive acts that they have demonstrated. It would be most unjust and against our sense of fairness, to condemn all of the Two-Leggeds, for the cruel actions of a few.

We are always delighted and happy to see the young children running about our woodlands. We watch them as they pick Bluebells for their mothers. When a flower is picked with love, the flower is happy, and so are we.

Please offer your help today because we need to restore peace and harmony to Bluebell copse. Speak to the Bluebell Farwellers, and they will tell you how you may help. Thank you for coming today."

It was with sad hearts, and tender hands, that the copse was cleared. The Bluebell clan went around to all the remaining Bluebells ensuring they were all in good condition, soothing them with gentle hands and magic words that the Abra had given them. When that was done, the Bluebell clan gave their thanks to all the helpers who had stayed and worked with them. Then slowly with heavy hearts, they sadly made their way back home.

"It's a pity we cannot explain to the Two-Leggeds how wrong it is to rip a plant from the earth, and heartlessly throw it away. How can we teach them that such actions cause pain and distress?" Scarletina asked her mother.

"Scarletina, it would be foolish and wrong to group all Two-Leggeds together. The Keeper of Peace and Tranquility said there are many who work with Mother Nature. They try to make things better. It is difficult for them to know how we feel, to understand how connected we are to the Earth. We respect everything, whether it be fairies, plants, insects, animals, or trees. Stones and pine cones deserve our respect and care. If something is part of our lives, then we honour it. Thankfully, there are many of the Two-Leggeds who feel as we do, and for that we must be grateful."

Scarletina asked her mother, "Why did they run away last night? I mean, they sounded really frightened!"

Her mother started laughing, "Oh, the Abra gave them quite a scare with the thick Mist. It came in very quickly; they couldn't see where they were going! They kept bumping into each other, and into the trees and bushes, too. Then, of course, the strange shapes and eerie noises within the Mist alarmed them. We don't think they will be coming back here again. Now, let us return home and cheer ourselves up; we will spend some time with your brother, Jagon."

The following morning Scarletina met Shantreel at their usual meeting place before walking to class. And, of course, they started talking about what had happened the day before. "It was awful, wasn't it Shantreel? So many of our beautiful Bluebells hurt and killed. I hope we don't have to see anything like that again."

Shantreel replied, "My mother said it has only occurred once before in her memory. So, Scarletina, let us pray that it won't happen again. She said the flowers that died would still be able to grow again next year. The Bluebell clans have special potions for such things that they get from the Abra. Next year, we will see all the flowers blooming together once more."

"I felt so sorry for the Bluebell Greeters having to hand their much loved flowers over to the Farewellers to be returned to the earth. I mean, it's been only a short time since they were welcoming them," said Scarletina.

They walked along in silence for a while, until Shantreel asked, "How is your brother? Is he really tiny? What did they name him?"

"He is called Jagon. Oh, he is very small, but he's a lot of fun. He already knows who I am, and called me Tina this morning. Mother said in a little while he'll be able to say Scarletina."

"How long before he starts walking?" asked Shantreel.

"Anytime in the next couple of days. Maybe even earlier as we are like the animals, aren't we? We learn to walk and talk very soon after we are born," Scarletina replied.

"I bet you wish we got our wings as quickly," giggled Shantreel.

"Why are you laughing? I don't think it is funny that we have to wait so long for them," snapped a cross Scarletina.

"I laughed because I knew you'd get irritable. You can't wait for your wings to sprout! You are so funny, Scarletina! You know they will show when you are ready and not before. It will be the same in the Moon Circle. Once we have learned all we have to learn, our wings will unfold. That will mean we graduate to the Sun Circle where we learn to fly." Shantreel hugged Scarletina. "It makes no sense to get upset about something you have no control over; it just makes life more miserable for you, and those around you."

"I know you are right, but I can't help but wonder, who will graduate to the Moon Circle before the end of this summer season?" Scarletina said.

"I don't know. It's hard because we aren't told what we have to learn to graduate. My mother says when the time is right, and we have completed the lessons of the Earth Circle, it will happen. She cannot tell me, nor can anyone else, what the lessons are as we are all unique."

"Oh well," laughed Scarletina. Her mood restored to its sunny outlook, "as Suntra-Spider would say, live in the present, enjoy the day, the future will come soon enough!"

Chapter Ten
Feeling Proud

When Scarletina and Shantreel arrived at the Earth Circle, they found all the Cropplets talking about the sad events at Bluebell copse. Everyone was shocked such a terrible thing could happen in their wood.

"Can I have your attention, please," called out Tutty-Grandhill, "I have let you chat longer this morning, so you could share your thoughts about the recent tragic events at Bluebell copse. I think it will be a good idea now if we put it to one side, and continue with today's class."

Returning to their places, the students waited for their teacher to speak. She said "Today, we are going to talk about the Guardians who have protected and supported you in the Earth Circle and how the Guardians change when you graduate to the Moon Circle."

An excited buzz went round the class. Could this mean that some were ready to move on the next level?

Scarletina saw Abradina and her brother, Abragan, look at each other, wondering perhaps if it was their turn. Shantreel gave her an excited grin to Scarletina. Even if it wasn't their turn, it would be so thrilling to see someone's wings sprout!

"We must also remember that the girls go to the Moon Circle, but the boys enter the Star Circle," said Tutty-Grandhill.

Shantreel raised her hand, "Yes," said her teacher, "what would you like to ask?"

"I wanted to know why we are separated. I mean, what do the boys do in the Star Circle that is different to what the girls do in our Moon Circle?"

Tutty-Grandhill responded, "One of the skills the boys learn is the art of defense and attack, which of course is only used as a last resort by us, but it has to be learned or the commune would be vulnerable."

"Why can't girls learn this?" questioned another student.

"They can," Tutty-Grandhill responded, "if they have shown promise in this field. As you know, we've had several physical challenges in the Earth Circle. We did this to see if any of the girls showed a talent for going into the defense class. No girl finished any of the Test of Endurance challenges. If anyone had, then she would have been offered the opportunity to go to the Star Circle, just for the art of defense and attack classes. Scarletina managed to be the first girl back in the TreeTop Chase Challenge. Her time was good, but she was five minutes behind the last boy."

"So what do the girls learn that we don't, then?" asked one of the boys.

"You need to change your way of thinking, Cropplets! It isn't about what the boys do versus what the girls do! However, there are certain things, for instance, that are only suitable for the girls such as learning about Fairy Motherhood. That really wouldn't be much fun for you boys now, would it? Also, if a Cropplet feels they want to learn an aspect of the other Circle, then they make a request to their teacher. The teacher will then approach the Circle Magnificents, who will consider the request. You are only separated for one circle. Once this is completed, you come back together again for the Sun Circle. Are there any more questions or can we move onto talking about our Guardians?

The room remained quiet. All were eager, and ready to hear about the Guardians, and possibly who might be joining the Moon Circle.

"Good, so let us begin," said Tutty-Grandhill. "One of the Spider-Clan has been with you whilst you've been a Cropplet. Because you cannot fly, your Guardian was allowed to hear your thoughts and feelings, so that they could protect and care for you. Their task was to keep you safe, and help you if you got into any trouble, which is something Cropplets seem to do quite a lot!"

The students giggled at this, and looked round to one another, knowing this was very true. There wasn't one of them that hadn't gotten themselves into some sort of mischief, and hadn't needed to be saved by their Spider-Clan Guardian.

"When you move to the Moon and Star Circle, you need to be more responsible. Your new Guardians will not be able to hear your thoughts as easily as your Spider Guardians have. You will have to learn the many different call signs of your Winged-Guardians. This will be your way of calling to them when they aren't with you and you need help. We cannot have you unprotected as you still cannot fly. The call for danger is the first one you will learn. You won't begin classes until you have mastered this."

"May I ask, Tutty-Grandhill, are there any students going to the Moon or Star Circle?" Darbetta bravely asked.

"Thank you for asking that, Darbetta. I do not know who the Cropplets are, but I have been told by the Magnificents that there are five Cropplets who will soon be ready to move to the Moon Circle. This is why they said it was time to speak about the new Guardians to you all.

Before becoming a Marvenor, the title for a student of the Moon Circle, each Cropplet has a Graduation Ritual to go through. The chosen students will wait here in the classroom. Their Spider-Clan Guardian goes through the Secret Handing Over Ceremony. This is where they release responsibility for their Cropplet and pass it onto the new Winged-Clan Guardian."

"Why do we have to change Guardians?" asked a student.

"Your needs alter as you grow, so the teachings and experiences you'll be learning in the next Circle are different from the ones you have learnt here. Therefore, you need a different kind of Guardian. The Winged-clan in the Moon Circle will take you up into the sky to get you used to looking down on the earth. It can be quite scary at first, but also great fun!" The Cropplets were amazed to see a huge grin on Tutty-Grandhill's face when she said this, showing how enjoyable it must be!

Scarletina and Shantreel looked at one another, a look that said they hoped they would both be graduating together. They made their sign of secret friends, tapping their chin twice with two fingers. Though they were starting to make new friends, there was a strong bond between them. They really wanted to be together, and share the new and exciting times in the Moon Circle.

Tutty-Grandhill let the Cropplets talk excitedly for a few minutes, before asking them to become still and quiet. She had another announcement to make on a very different matter. "I would like Scarletina Oak-Sharder to come to the front of the class." Scarletina's face showed shock, surprise, and dismay. What had she done now?

"Face the class, Scarletina," ordered Tutty-Grandhill.

Everyone was silent, and all eyes were on Scarletina. Facing the class meant something serious was going to be said. Tutty-Grandhill continued, "As you know, Scarletina's brother, Jagon, was welcomed the night before the Sadness at Bluebell Copse happened. Whilst waiting in the Queen-Beech tree, Scarletina became worried and fearful for the safety of her brother. She believed the fairies from Blackdown Wood were going to try to steal some of the Downies!"

The students reacted just as Tutty-Grandhill knew they would as all had heard a little about the Blackdown fairies, and how they had tried to steal Downies. Holding up her hand for quiet, she continued, "Scarletina, though very frightened, went to the entrance of the Queen-Beech tree to see if they were there. This took great courage on her part. Her love for her brother, and all the other Downies, made her brave enough to look for the Blackdown fairies. Thankfully, it was a false alarm. I would like all of you to show Scarletina how proud we are that she showed such bravery and courage."

Tutty-Grandhill led the class, who showed their appreciation, in the usual fairy way. Everyone raised their hands above their heads, linked their fingers, and rocked their enclosed hands back and forth, while whilst chanting Choo-Hah Choo-Hah Choo-Hah.

Scarletina happily responded with the Fairy Thank You. With her wrists together, she tapped her fingers against each other, and bowed her head three times. She smiled at everyone, very thankful that she wasn't in any trouble.

Suddenly, Scarletina felt a light tingling in her back, it was like a feather tickling her. No matter how she tried, she couldn't manage to scratch it. Twisting and turning, she squirmed and wriggled, but it wasn't any use. She couldn't reach it. And the itching got worse!

"Whatever is the matter, Scarletina?" asked Tutty-Grandhill.

"Oh, I have such an itch, and I can't reach it!" Her fellow Cropplets were laughing as they watched Scarletina; she looked so funny, writhing and jumping around trying to scratch her back.

"Let me help you," offered her teacher, and pulled the tunic open at the back, "Oh, I see what the problem is."

"Whatever is it? I have never had such an itch before," asked Scarletina.

"Class, please stand and welcome our first, Marvenor. Scarletina Oak-Sharder, your wings have begun to sprout. Congratulations, you are our first Cropplet ready to graduate to the Moon Circle."

Chapter Eleven
Five Of Us

Scarletina proudly showed her newly formed wing buds to her classmates. She felt very excited, yet a little afraid as she was now a Marvenor, a student of the Moon Circle. She had longed for this moment, and yet now it was here, she sadly realised it meant leaving her dear friends, and the familiar ways of the Earth Circle.

"Congratulations, Scarletina! I am so thrilled you are the first to graduate. Your parents will be very proud of you." Shantreel hugged her friend close, but she was also having mixed feelings. Happy that her best friend would be moving onto the Moon Circle, but sad because they were being parted.

"You will be next, Shantreel, I just know it. I couldn't bear being parted from you; it wouldn't be the same," replied a somewhat tearful Scarletina.

Abradina and her brother, Abragan, came over to offer their congratulations, too. "How are you feeling, Scarletina?" Abradina asked.

"Excited, but a little bit scared and sad, too. It's going to a big change for me, and don't forget I still have the final test to take."

"Well, I am sure you felt the same way when you first started in the Earth Circle, and look at the friends you have made, and the fun you have had. It will be the same in the Moon Circle. You will soon be making new friends. The final test will be all right. I don't think I have ever heard of a Cropplet failing it."

"Yes, Abradina, you are right, but I hope that some of my friends graduate, too; it would make it a lot better for me," admitted Scarletina.

Tutty-Grandhill asked everyone to be seated, and asked if there were any questions. One of the Cropplets said, "What will Scarletina do now? I mean, when does she graduate and go to the Moon Circle?"

"That is a good question to ask. Scarletina will take the final test, if she passes, she will be ready to graduate. At the Graduation Ritual, Scarletina will receive her new tunic. Cropplets wear green, but the Marvenor's colour is silver. Of course, it is also slightly different at the back as space has to be given for the wing buds. She will meet her new Winged-Clan Guardian. Once everything is done, she will move onto the Moon Circle."

Shantreel asked, "You said that there were five Cropplets due to graduate. Will this happen soon? I mean... I think that Scarletina would be happier if she had some company from the Earth Circle when she starts her new class."

"Shantreel, I cannot answer that question as I do not know when a student's wings are going to bud. Sometimes I wish I did for it would make my life a lot easier. It is kind of you to think of your friend, but she is ready to graduate to the Moon Circle, so she has to go," Tutty-Grandhill replied.

Scarletina did the secret friends sign, tapping two fingers on her chin, to Shantreel, who did the same back. But her eyes were full of tears, which slowly started to trickle down her face.

"Why are you crying, Shantreel?" Tutty-Grandhill asked.

"I am just feeling sad for Scarletina. Oh, I am so pleased her wings have budded, but I was hoping that she would have some friends joining her when she left. I think it is going to be hard for her starting a new class on her own."

"And you were thinking that you are the one who should be joining her?" asked her teacher.

"Oh no, Tutty-Grandhill, no! I wasn't thinking of anyone in particular. I just thought it would be nicer for Scarletina to have a friend to share this new beginning with."

"You have a kind heart, Shantreel, and think of others. You have been a very good friend to Scarletina, Indeed, I think you may have prevented her from getting into more trouble with your wise words. She will miss you and your influence."

Shantreel blushed, and started to speak, when she jumped up from her seat and screamed "Oh, I have something crawling down my back! Help me get it out, please!"

Scarletina rushed over and looked inside her friend's tunic, she shouted, "You have wing buds Shantreel! You have wing buds!"

The friends held each other tightly, each feeling the wing buds on the other's back. Tears of joy and happiness flowed from their eyes as they realised they would be going to the Moon Circle together!

Suddenly, Darbetta, Abradina, and Abragan leapt to their feet as they felt their wings starting to bud. The class watched and laughed at the three of them jumping and wriggling around. Then the three looked at each other's backs to see the buds, and finally held one another as they shared this wonderful moment.

"Class, we now know the five Cropplets who will be moving to the Moon Circle. Let us congratulate them all."

Chapter Twelve
Flying High

Scarletina tossed and turned in her bed; she was wide awake, so decided to creep out onto the branches, as her mother had earlier suggested.

"You have had a very exciting day, little one, so you may find it hard to sleep. It is a very mild night, so if that happens, go outside and sit for a while. Stay very close though."

It had been such a wonderful day, made even more special when her friends wings budded. They would all start at the Moon Circle together. Her eyes had become used to the darkness, so she easily saw Suntra-Spider making her way along the branches.

The spider wrapped several of her long legs around Scarletina, gently touching her wing buds and whispered, "I am so proud of you, little one".

"Thank you, Suntra-Spider, but I couldn't have done it without all your help. Thank you so much for always being there for me. Will you still be taking me to the Moon Circle?"

"No, I won't, as I will have a new Cropplet to take care of! You will have one of the Winged-Clan take you."

Scarletina started to cry, "But I need you, Suntra-Spider. What will I do without you? Who will I have to help and guide me with wise words?"

"Hush now, don't cry. Everything will be all right. I promise, and I have never broken a promise to you, have I? This is the way of things. You are growing up, and you need a different kind of Guardian. I will always be thinking of you, and watching from afar."

"If I need you, can I ask you to come and visit me?" whispered Scarletina.

"No, Scarletina, that wouldn't be fair to my new Cropplet, now would it? I want you to know that you have been very special to me. I am so proud to have been your Guardian and to have been a part of your life. It is time for us to go our different ways, and for you to get to know your new Guardian."

"Do you know who it is?" asked Scarletina.

"Yes, I do, and I know that you two will work well together. We will be meeting tomorrow after class. You and the other four Cropplets will take your final test and

I will attend the handing over ceremony. I must go now, little one. Sleep well, and I will see you in the morning."

Scarletina watched her dear, and much loved, Guardian, disappear into the darkness. She would miss her company and wise guidance so much. Life was going to be very different, but now, it seemed more exciting than scary, and that pleased Scarletina.

The class was empty except for four nervous Cropplets who were seated at their desks. Darbetta, Shantreel, Abradina and Scarletina were waiting to meet their new Guardians. Abragan had already gone to the Star Circle to meet his new Guardian and continue his studies.

The Cropplets were not allowed to see the handing over ceremony because the Abra Clan were there. Special secret spells had to be done to ensure that all connections were cut between the Cropplets and their Spider-Clan Guardians.

The Cropplets had taken the final test that morning. The test papers had been written specifically for each individual. They were all very relieved when Tutty-Grandhill told them they'd all passed.

She had also suggested that while they were waiting for the ceremony to finish that they bring their Personal Quest Diaries up to date. All of them had enjoyed writing about their wings budding, and the happiness they shared about graduating together. They also wrote of their gratitude to their teacher, for her knowledge, and patience. Scarletina, Shantreel and Darbetta thanked each of their Spider-Guardians for always being there with their wise guidance and encouragement. Abradina was not permitted to reveal the name of her Abra Guardian, so she simply wrote, 'Thank you, Guardian. You will forever be in my heart'.

Suddenly, four of the Winged-Clan came into the classroom. There was Raven, Blue Jay, Kingfisher and Mistle Thrush, and each Marvenor was thinking the same thought: which one of them was her Guardian?

Tutty-Grandhill said when their names were called out, they were to come to the front of the class. They would be given their new tunic, and introduced to their Guardian.

Darbetta's was called out first, and her Guardian was Kesra-Kingfisher. This was perfect for her as he fished from the rivers and streams that her clan looked after. His feathers of blue, white, and orange, shone brightly. His long beak held Darbetta's tunic, which he gently handed to her.

Rethna-Raven was Abradina's Guardian. Not only were his feathers all black, but so were his beak, legs, and feet. He had shaggy feathers under his beak, too. Lifting her tunic from Tutty-Grandhill's open hand, Rethna-Raven offered it to her.

☘

Next Shantreel was called out to meet Mavina-Mistle Thrush, who had dark brown spots on her creamy coloured belly, and always filled the woods with her melodious singing. Even when the weather was bad and stormy, she still sang. Softly, she placed Shantreel's tunic into her open hands, and sang for her.

That left Jadakina-Jackdaw as Scarletina's Guardian. His silvery white coloured eyes, followed her as she made her way to the front of the classroom. She saw he had silver coloured feathers on his back and neck, but the rest of him was dark grey. He stared at her for a few moments before he lifted her tunic from the table, and placed it firmly in her hands.

"The ceremony is complete, your time in the Earth Circle is over," said Tutty-Grandhill, "you have worked very hard in my class, and I am proud to have been able to teach you. I hope you will continue to learn, and enjoy your time in the Moon Circle. You may spend a few minutes collecting your belongings, then your new Guardians will take you home."

"That means we will be flying home! Oh my goodness that is so exciting!" Scarletina whispered to the others.

"Aren't our tunics beautiful, such a lovely colour, I will be able to adorn mine with some very pretty things," said Shantreel as she emptied her desk.

"I am so thrilled to be graduating with you all. If I was going to be on my own, I don't think I would be looking forward to it as much," confided Darbetta.

"My clan will be very happy, as Ravens are known for their wisdom, and healing ways," said Abradina.

Before they left, all four Cropplets stood before their teacher, and did the Cropplets thank you ritual. They raised their arms above their heads, hands clasped together, with their fingers intertwined, and rocked their enclosed hands back and forth whilst chanting Choo-Hah Choo-Hah Choo-Hah. Tutty-Grandhill responded with the fairy thank you ritual, placing her wrists together, she tapped her fingers against each other, and bowed her head three times.

Tutty-Grandhill then led Scarletina, Shantreel, Abradina and Darbetta to their Guardians. The birds crouched low so each Marvenor could climb up them, by gripping onto their feathers. Though Darbetta did it differently, she climbed onto Kesra-Kingfishers beak, and then onto his back.

"Hold on tightly all of you! Take it gently with them Guardians! No diving or aerobatics today, we don't want them falling off," called Tutty-Grandhill.

Jadakina-Jackdaw asked, "Are you ready Scarletina Marvenor?"

Taking a deep breath, and holding on as tightly as she could, Scarletina answered, "I am ready Jadakina-Jackdaw."

Soon they were high above Nightingale Wood, and the wind was pulling at Scarletina's hair, and blowing it into her eyes, but she was too scared to let go and push it away. Scarletina was frightened, but at the same time, loving the thrill of flying. It wasn't like anything she had ever done before.

" Scarletina Marvenor, you are very brave, so I think we are going to get along very well. I see Shard, so our journey is coming to an end. I will land on the branch close to your home."

"Thank you Jadakina-Jackdaw and I wish we could fly for longer, but I know my family will be waiting to hear about today."

Her new Guardian made a smooth landing and waited for Scarletina to get down, then said to her, "I will be here at the usual school time to take you to the Moon Circle. It is further than the Earth Circle, but you will not be walking, so we do not need to leave earlier. I think we have many adventures ahead of us Scarletina Marvenor. All I ask, is that you are always honest with me, even if you feel that I might be displeased with you, I always want to know the truth."

Scarletina hooked her thumbs together, so that she could make the Winged-Oath. Her Guardian gave a nod of satisfaction, "I know that your Winged-Oath is never broken, so I am happy that you have taken it."

With those final words, her Guardian effortlessly took flight, soaring high into the sky. He gave an amazing display of dives and twists and turns, showing Scarletina, that fairies weren't the only ones who were good at aerobatics.

Scarletina sat on the branch for a while, she needed some quiet time to think about all that had happened during the day. Her wings had budded! She had her new tunic, and an amazing new Guardian. Best of all, her three friends would be with her in the Moon Circle.

Any fear she had felt, was gone. She was excited at the changes the future held. She couldn't wait to begin her new adventures in the Moon Circle, with her friends Shantreel, Abradina, Darbetta and her new Guardian, Jadakina-Jackdaw.

Author
Bess Drew Sherret

Bess Drew Sherret is a natural storyteller who enjoys entertaining children with all sorts of creative tales, many of which contain a positive message. As a child, Bess was drawn to nature, and her passion for bugs and plants and other woodland critters is reflected in *Scarletina's Quest for Fairy Wings*. She has found that children are more open to hearing about doing the right thing when the lessons are woven into a fantasy setting. Bess decided to combine her talents for storytelling with her beliefs about respecting people, plants, and animals to help children understand that we are responsible for everything we say and do. As a result, Scarletina has adventures that allow children to see that everyone—whether human or fairy—must accept the positive and negative outcomes for their words and actions.

Bess spent many hours researching and learning about the flora and fauna featured in the book to make sure all of the details were correct. When she is not studying nature or spending time outdoors, she designs and makes jewelry and has enjoyed performing in theatre productions for many years. She also enjoys cooking and attending Calgary Hitmen hockey games. She lives in Silver Spring, Calgary, with her husband, Alex.

bessdrewsherret.ca

Printed in Canada